Seeing Through Snow

Matthew Higgins

Seeing Through Snow

Seeing Through Snow
ISBN 978 1 76041 389 7
Copyright © Matthew Higgins 2017
Front cover: Children on skis at Kiandra, c.1906,
photograph by Charles Kerry or Charles Plumb (National
Library of Australia PIC Cold Store #PIC/18228)
Back cover: A change in the weather, Snowy Mountains,
2016, photograph by Matthew Higgins
Internal pen and pencil drawings: found in a sketchbook kept by Les Leong

First published 2017 by
GINNINDERRA PRESS
PO Box 3461 Port Adelaide 5015
www.ginninderrapress.com.au

The following stories were recorded in a series of oral history interviews with former Kiandra resident Les Leong. By the time I met Les, he was living in the Tumut Nursing Home and was aged in his late 80s. He was a kind old man who generously shared with me his memories of life in an earlier Australia, an Australia very different to the one I knew. He also had a quirky way of looking at things, and some of his experiences were well and truly out of the ordinary. Luckily for me, Les was also very frank, and he was willing to talk about all aspects of his life, even quite personal things. Les had attempted to write up parts of his life story, and sometimes read the chapters aloud to me during the recording sessions. At other times, he spoke straight from memory. The interviews were conducted for the National Library of Australia and you can listen to the recordings at the library.

Les died last year, shortly after the interviews were completed. His siblings were all gone by then, as were most of his old friends, so it was a lonely funeral at the Tumut Cemetery. Fittingly, just as Les came into the world during a blizzard, it was snowing the day he went into the ground. As the clods of earth rattled onto his casket, I vowed to publish his story. It was the least I could do for a man who had shared so much with me. A bushman, Les was nonetheless educated and spoke well; although I've had to clean up his speech a little, the narrative is pretty authentic to his voice. I hope that you find his story as compelling as I do.

Rowley Pendergast

Canberra, 1982

The spelling of Kosciuszko in this book uses the old form (without the modern 'z') as that is the spelling that was used in Les's era.

'Memoir is not an act of history but an act of memory, which is innately corrupt.' – Mary Karr, poet and memoirist (b. 1955)

'Life is like a landscape. You live in the midst of it, but can describe it only from the vantage point of distance.' – Charles A. Lindbergh, aviator and author (1902–1974)

1

Somewhere in the howl of the morning blizzard there was another sound.

Mrs Edie Leong pricked up her ears. 'Shoosh,' she said to the squabbling brood of kids that was running around in the kitchen of the slab hut.

Edie concentrated and turned towards the rough door of the hut. The noise seemed to be coming from outside. Edie walked towards the door. Just then a particularly strong wind gust blew over the hut, sending snowdrift down the kitchen chimney and hissing into the fire. Flames spluttered under the cook pot where the family's porridge was bubbling. But Edie didn't notice. She was already sure she knew what the sound was. It was a baby.

Edie grasped the battered doorknob and swung open the door. Looking down, she almost couldn't believe what she saw. Wrapped in a small dirty blanket fitted into an old wooden soapbox was a tiny infant. Edie grabbed the bawling child and took it inside. Cradling the bundle in her arms, she rushed to the fireplace, and knelt down to warm the almost blue flesh.

'What is it?' chorused the four children, whose attention was now riveted on their mother.

'It's a poor, tiny child. But where's her mother?' she said as much to herself as to Jim, Peter, Mary and Belle. 'What on earth has happened here?' Edie mumbled, verging on tears.

She and the children all looked down into the face of the baby, whose cries were slowly dissipating in the warmth of the hut. The baby looked up at his rescuers, blinking away the last of the snowflakes from its face.

That baby was me.

2

Yep, I owe my life to Edie and Tom Leong. Though of course I don't remember that day when Mrs Leong (mum) picked me up outside her home during the big blizzard of '91, I've formed a picture of it in my mind, formed from all the times I've been told it. Apparently I was seconds away from freezing, but a good pair of lungs brought rescue, and I've never looked back.

The Leongs, part of the Chinese-Australian community in our little town, immediately became heroes that day. By the time word was sent to Tom at his general store, half the town already knew. 'The miracle of Poverty Hill' (for Poverty Hill was the unprepossessing part of Kiandra in which we lived) even made it into the Cooma newspaper.

Kiandra's two policemen, usually occupied with desultory cases of drunkenness, theft, assault or accidental death in the surrounding mineshafts or winter snowdrifts, now tried to identify the mystery mother who'd abandoned her child. But after weeks of investigation they came up with nothing. In such a small community, it is hard to believe that a pregnancy could have been concealed for so long. But that seems to be what happened. Given the voluminous dresses that women wore in those times, maybe hiding an expanding abdomen might not have been so hard. Certainly the mother wasn't an outsider, for the coaches had been stopped at the beginning of that winter and the only way to get into Kiandra was on snowshoes (or what you call skis today). A heavily pregnant woman on snowshoes certainly would not have gone unnoticed!

So I became child number five in the Leong home.

3

My stepfather (a funny word we never used at home – Tom was just Dad – but in my travels I've met people who thought it unacceptable that I should have a Chinese-descent 'Dad') owed his life and happiness to that deep belief among Chinese in luck.

His father, Ah Sam Leong, had come to Kiandra during the rush in 1860. He was part of a 'human carting convoy', a team of carriers employed to bring in goods for the Anglo storekeepers. They worked like slaves in all sort of conditions; once the team was caught in a blizzard five miles short of Kiandra and half of them got frostbitten feet. Ah Sam, one of very few Chinese to come to the goldfields from mountainous Gansu province in western China instead of the more common Canton or Guangzhou area, had some experience of snow and had taken care to wear extra footwear. He ended up carrying one of his companions on his shoulders. The injured man had his stinking, gangrenous foot amputated inside the Kiandra doctor's tent on a bare table. Doc's rusty old saw probably hadn't been cleaned in a while. A doctor's tent on a mining field isn't so different to a butcher's shambles. The patient died of infection within a week.

That was Ah Sam's first escape. The second time providence smiled on him was after he'd bought his way out of the carrying team and joined a Chinese mining party. After getting good gold in Pollocks Gully, the party fell on hard times and decided to move on – minus Ah Sam who, despite the poor gold, seemed to like Kiandra. The rest of the party unfortunately chose the Burrangong field, where Young is today.

Shortly after they arrived, the white miners rioted there at Lambing Flat, stormed the Chinese camp at Blackguards Gully in a heated rush of racial frenzy and violently assaulted many Chinese. Grandfather's former friends were found among the beaten, minus their pigtails and with gaping head wounds.

Grandfather Leong kept a low profile in Kiandra, but gradually a form of acceptance of racial difference developed in the town. Maybe that was because there were relatively few Chinese in Kiandra – certainly a lot less than over at Lambing Flat. The 'yellow threat' that so often aggrieved the whites simply didn't exist here. So much so that in October 1868 grandfather married a local woman, Agnes Prince. Together they ran a butchery followed by a guest house and became respected members of the goldfield's business community. By now known as Sam Leong, Granddad became wealthy enough to lend money to people – white and Chinese alike – and so had fingers in all sorts of town pies. Some of them were particularly tasty ones.

Sam also led the Chinese contingent at the annual snowshoe races for which the town became quite famous in its day. Sydney photographer Charles Kerry (who I met many times) took brilliant pictures of these events later around 1900, but Sam had been racing on the 'demon showshoes' for years before that. And as his children got older, they became famous skiers too. Dad, born in 1870, did the fastest time down Township Hill as a six-year-old. *The Sydney Morning Herald* even noted his feat, but evidently didn't notice the Chinese connection, as he was named in the article Tom Long. Many of the miners then still used the sluice box called a Long Tom, so Dad was nicknamed Long Tom Leong and when he set up his own store had business cards printed with the name, a name which he wore as a badge of Kiandra honour.

4

Grandmother Agnes had her own interesting history. The surname was certainly ironic – her family was anything but princely. Her father Sean (my great grandfather) had come out as a convict from Ireland, and in time became quite a good stockman, working for squatters the Delaroys over around Cooma. Those who knew him said he had few rivals on horseback. He could ride the wildest horse and won all the local gymkhanas. Some of the things he could do were almost like ballet. He could gallop along a course and pick up a hat from the ground, could jump up on the saddle at full gallop and ride without reins. People round about all said he was superb – given the way mountain folk prize riding prowess, that's saying a lot. But he had a liking for the rum and got reported for drunkenness.

So he took off for some time and lived with Aborigines in the Monaro – outcasts together – and learned all his bush skills from them. These Ngarigo men were pretty impressive in the bush – well, they'd lived there for generations of course. They taught him how to hunt bush animals and make all sorts of things from hides – whether it was possum, kangaroo or quoll. Sean got to know the bush trails too; way up into the mountains they'd go in the summer. It wasn't just to eat those bogong moths either, but they'd have ceremonies and trade with other groups. Old Sean was usually left out of that sort of thing, but he certainly came to know a lot about the blacks' way of life.

Eventually he was able to come back into white society, but in the meantime he'd started living with one of the Ngarigo women, who's always been known in the family as Bella. Sean and Bella built a slab and bark hut on another of the big runs, as Sean by now was a handy bushman. Being able to get on well with the blacks, he was a valuable go-between for his employers, who constantly feared the blacks spearing their sheep and cattle.

Sean knew of many battles between squatters and the tribes over stock spearing. He was dead by the time I was adopted by Edie and Tom, but I've heard Dad talk about several sites where Ngarigo men were killed by stockmen and their bodies burned to destroy the evidence. There's a place where Right Hand Creek joins the Murrumbidgee out towards Long Plain where there used to be skulls and jawbones visible on the ground amongst the soil and half-washed-away ashes. It was a terribly harsh frontier. Many of the stories I don't like to remember.

Sean and Bella had a lot of kids, most of whom died. Heaps of kids never made it beyond a few months in those days, living in rough huts, no hygiene, miles from doctors. But Agnes must have been a toughie and she survived diphtheria and falls from horses and wasp stings and what not and grew into an attractive young woman.

Having come from this mixed-blood background, she had no qualms about marrying a Chinese. Especially one as canny as Ah Sam Leong.

5

I mentioned that Granddad had some interesting business ventures. He abhorred opium, which he believed had wrecked too many Chinamen in Australia, but he was not averse to whisky. Spirits, especially baijiu or grain spirit, were part of the Chinese culture. But of course the cost of bringing them into Kiandra was pretty prohibitive. So Grandfather decided to make his own. He was as clever as a snake, and as slippery as one too sometimes. I guess that's how he stayed out of the clutches of the law.

The distilling season was short, owing to the cold winters preventing year-round operation of the stills he had hidden out in the snowgum-studded hills. So he had to make the most of his opportunities and that meant he was very jealous of his illicit trade. When he found out that one of the town's other Chinese, Ah Ket, was also stilling, Grandfather decided to do something about it. Some called Grandfather ruthless, but he had a sense of humour too.

The way old Sam told the story, he crept into Ah Ket's camp one morning after Ket had gone into town. Of course, all the Chinese kept pigs, as pork was part of their regular diet. One of the constant sources of friction between Chinese and Anglos in Kiandra was about pigs and the stink they caused and the way they'd root up people's gardens if they got out. Anyway, Granddad grabbed one of Ah Ket's pigs and tied it up by the rear legs to a wire fence just behind Ket's little hut.

When Ah Ket came home, he hears this pig squealing and goes to investigate. He sees his prize porker hanging from the fence and runs over to release it. Granddad had set a snare trap for Ket – Ket puts his foot in the loop of No. 8 fencing wire hidden in leaves on the ground and – whoosh – he's grabbed by the ankle and flung upside down on the wire that Sam had tied to this bent sapling!

So, here's Ah Ket upside down, next to his prize pig, and both of them squealing. Granddad of course is behind a tree and now appears with a carving knife. Apparently Ket was so terrified – he immediately knew what Granddad was there about – that he peed himself on the spot. All this piss running down his shirt and dripping off his upside-down face.

Granddad simply walked up to him, gently pushed the tip of the blade against Ket's throat and said, 'No more still.'

Granddad had no trouble with Ah Ket after that. Ket was walking on crutches for weeks afterwards, but no matter how many times people asked him, he wouldn't tell how he'd injured his ankle.

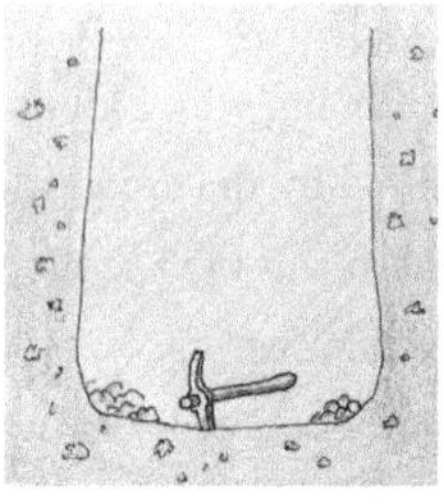

6

Speaking of injuries, growing up in a bush town like that, us kids had plenty of scrapes when we were young. My worst one was when I was about six. And it was all to do with sister Mary's stupid possum.

One day when Dad had been getting firewood with some of the other town men, he felled this dead snowgum. It was a beauty with tons of dead wood, well-seasoned, which would make a good heap of fuel. As the tree crashed to the ground, this possum bounced out of one of the hollows in the trunk. It wasn't a brushtail, but a bobuck, which is the kind you get in the high country. It seemed a bit groggy, but otherwise uninjured. Usually Dad never took us little kids on these sorts of trips because he thought it was too dangerous; mostly it was Jim and Peter who got to go, as they were a bit older and at least a bit more sensible (though with Peter I used to wonder sometimes, as you'll see later). But on this day, for some reason Mary was there too.

Of course, as soon as she saw the possum ricochet out of the tree, she raced over to it and picked it up. 'Can we take it home?' she pleaded to Dad.

'No'.'

'Oh please, please'

'No.'

'Please, Daddy, pleeeease.'

After about ten minutes of this, Dad just gave up and Mary had a new pet.

Possums are notorious for biting and scratching – normally you'd never try to pick one up, but this one was young, maybe just out of the pouch. Mary fed it and it became a part of the family. It generally lived up in the rafters of the house, sleeping by day and active by night. As it grew older, Mum became less enamoured of it when it started knocking over tins of flour and sugar, so it was 'encouraged' to live outside. It then took up residence in a tree near the back door and we'd say hello to it of a morning when we got up and it went to bed.

Well, one day a neighbour's dog was sniffing around the place – back in those times few people kept their dogs under any sort of control and loose dogs were commonplace. It came to the tree and looking up suddenly saw this possum. It went into a fit and jumped and barked like it was mad. Bob the possum woke with a start and made a leap for another tree. The leaping dog followed, and Bob kept going. Soon it ran out of trees and made a bid for escape across the ground. The crazed dog raced behind and just as it was about to crunch Bob in its jaws, the bloody possum dived down this old mineshaft down towards the creek.

Of course, Mary had heard the commotion, as had I, and we'd been following. By this time Mary, who wasn't much older than me, was in hysterics. Little though I was, I thought I'd be the brotherly hero, so I threw some stones at the dog as it pranced around the top of the shaft. The third one hit it right on the nose and the hound ran off squealing. I was chuffed, but that still left the possum down the hole. Mary was bawling so I decided to climb down the shaft to rescue Bob.

Being only six, to me that shaft looked like it was a mile deep. But I started climbing down nevertheless. Then after only a few yards my footing slipped and down I went. Right to the bottom. What I didn't know was that the shaft was still in use. Old Sailor, a recluse who lived on the edge of town, had been down there fossicking and had left his pick stuck in the bottom of the shaft. One part of the pick's head was in the ground while the other was sticking straight up. As I hit the bottom, my right hand went straight onto that pick point, and the pick went straight through me hand!

So I was pinned to the ground by my hand. All the commotion
had brought Mother to the top of the shaft and when she saw what
had happened she almost died. But having great presence of mind,
she quickly got help and someone or other came down the shaft and
rescued me. But he had to carry me up with the pick still through my
hand.

That's how the doctor saw me when he got to our place some little
time later. Doc was able to pull the pick out and he did a good job
with stitches; luckily none of the ligaments were torn. But I've had this
scar in my right hand ever since. From that time on, Father O'Brien,
Kiandra's Catholic priest, used to joke about the stigmata, calling me
Little Jesus. Possibly sacrilegious, yes, but Father was a good-humoured
man and every Easter if he saw me he'd give me a wink. Once, we did
a nativity scene at school as part of a Christmas celebration. You can
guess who was in the crib!

You can still see the scar in my right hand from that pick – look,
see there? I have a scar on my left hand too, but that's another story
for later.

7

Old Sailor was one of the old hands – one of the diggers who'd come to Kiandra during the main rush back in 1860. My father told me that Sailor had earlier been a stockman and had been among the earliest white men to enter the Kiandra area back when the first cattle were brought up here in the late 1830s. That was when the place was called Gibsons Plains, after Andrew Gibson, the squatter who sent those cattle up. Until the men got to know how treacherous the weather could be here, many cattle died in the snowdrifts when early blizzards blew in before stock could be got down out of the high country. Sailor told father all sorts of stories like that – carcasses caught up in the branches of trees, so deep was the snow, you know.

So, he must have been close to ninety by the time of that pick incident. Amazing that a man who had lived such a tough life could live to that ripe old age. Unfortunately by the time I become an adult and started showing an interest in the past, Sailor was dead.

No one seems to know Sailor's real name, but he was certainly a convict, sent out for seven years and then granted his ticket of leave and eventually his conditional pardon and his freedom. Like most of those sorts of men, sent out for some small crime or other, if they had any sense they saw the opportunity that they had here in New South Wales and worked well for their employers. Provided the employer was reasonable, it wasn't all that long before men were free and looking to get their own stock and a piece of land. But of course with the squatters so well entrenched, little blokes like Sailor were sort of locked out and it took years for the land laws to change. That's why men like Sailor came to the goldfields – it was a real opportunity for independence.

Sailor had no maritime experience as far as I know. His nickname had a lot to do with that old Australian love of irony. Sailor apparently loathed washing. His skin was usually caked with dirt and his clothes always looked greasy. You could smell him from a hundred yards, so they say. 'The dirtiest man in the mountains.' He was even made by one of the town's publicans to drink outside! So they named him Sailor, because he so hated water.

Early in the town's history, when the rush was underway, it was nearly all men here. There were very few women. Blokes like Sailor, working in the bush with stock and that, had hardly ever spent time with women anyway, so a goldfield wasn't much different. By the time women started living here and the place became a bit civilised, Sailor was no longer a young man. His bachelor ways were set for life. So he lived in a little slab hut with a calico and bark roof (galvanised iron was too flash for him), making do with just the bare necessities. Talk about tough! You try living that way, especially when snow is three feet thick on the ground. Living on salt meat and damper, and a few vegetables when you could get them or grow them in the precious little summertime. Not letting on despite injuries down shafts that would make your hair stand on end just to hear about them. Broken ribs, fingers, and worse. He always dragged one foot when he walked – that too was from some mining accident; or was it a fall from a horse when he was young? – anyway, he always left this peculiar footprint behind him. But of course he had his rum bottle. That was his medicine, and that was his wife too. A little bit of colour in the pan from time to time kept Sailor going. The gold and the rum were his meaning in this cold life.

8

Most of the men in Kiandra drank to some extent. Rum was the choice, always. It packed a punch in one bottle that six bottles of beer wouldn't equal. Some men could hold their liquor but others couldn't. Sometimes that led to tragedy. There were a few men known as 'street angels and home devils' around our town.

One was Ted Smithers. He seemed an ordinary sort of bloke when you talked to him. Quite likeable really. But at home, and on the rum, he was a different person. His wife Jeannie put up with something awful. Shouting, threats, even beatings. My mother used to talk with dad over the dinner table about how she'd seen Mrs Smithers in the street and how she had bruises or a blackened eye. Mrs S increasingly had a haunted look about her as life drew on. The Smithers kids were always skittish too, like they were afraid something bad was about to happen.

The Smithers' house was a little way out of town, say a couple of miles. It was a tumbledown weatherboard affair with loose corrugated iron on the roof. Whenever you went past it on a windy day, you'd hear the iron sheets banging away. Real ramshackle. I don't know how they managed to live there, especially Mrs S, with all that was going on. And of course, being a bit away from town and a bit isolated, that only made it worse when Ted was in one of his rages. It wasn't easy for Mrs S to summon help when things were bad.

Then one day it reached a climax. The story got around town that the doctor had been called to the Smithers' place. Soon after, when Doc James returned to his surgery, the police met him there and there was a discussion. They then went down to the Smithers' house and questioned Ted for hours. But nothing came of it and certainly no arrest was made.

A few days later, Mrs Smithers was in the street. She was now blind in one eye and there was a terrible burn scar on her face. She told Mum that the fat she'd been cooking the breakfast in had splattered suddenly and hit her face. That was the public story but hardly anyone believed it. Most of the people had a fair idea that Ted had thrown the hot fat at her in one of his drunken rages. Without evidence, or any statement from Jeannie about what had really happened, the police were hamstrung.

There were a few tragic families like that one scattered among the hills. And of course the kids in those families were traumatised before they got very old. So that just sets up another generation of heartache and trouble. It sets seed that sooner or later is going to burst out in something terrible.

9

When I was a kid, there was a lot of hydraulic sluicing going on. That's where the miners cut a water race across the hills to run the water to a big iron nozzle which shoots the water at high pressure against the slopes to sluice out the gold-bearing dirt. Those races were a lot of fun for us kids when the water was running in them. We'd make little boats out of anything we had at hand. I was lucky because Dad had a soldering iron that he used to use on tinsmithing in the shop (you know, making billies and that sort of thing) and he'd make little tin boats for me.

I used to do pretty well in those races and we'd all make bets on who'd win. Usually it was for a handful of marbles or lollies or something. One day, one of the Smithers boys was there. We used to call him Butch because he was always wanting to fight you. See, this is what I meant about the influence of his father.

Well, on this day, my boat was cruising along the race, yards in front of the other kids' boats. Then Butch suddenly picks my boat out of the water and hurls it down the hill. I saw red and I rushed him. I was all sudden anger, but of course the sneaky little bastard had planned it and was ready for me. He just let go with this one punch right into my stomach and I was sent flying. He stomped on my boat and tramped off. The other kids didn't risk tackling him, and I didn't really blame them.

For months, I hated Butch Smithers for that. He only made it worse by always sneering at me and calling me Chinky or some other nasty word (of course I didn't look Chinese but having a Chinese-Australian family made me vulnerable to anyone of that racialist bent – luckily, there weren't many like that in Kiandra).

It was only a long time afterwards, and after lots of counselling by my wise old dad and mum that I learned to forgive Butch. I came to pity him and his siblings for what they obviously endured in their lonely horrible house.

The last time I heard about Butch he was still serving time in Goulburn Gaol for an armed hold-up somewhere around Michelago about 1920. There's a piece in the Bible about sowing and reaping. The trouble is that it's sometimes someone else who reaps what has been sown.

10

I haven't said much about my mother's family. Just as Dad came from an interesting mix, so did Mum. Edie's father, Walter Brickhill, was a run-of-the-mill Englishman who'd come out here as a surveyor back in the 1850s. He walked all over the bush with his chainmen and labourers. Of course at that time the bush was still really wild in many places and it wasn't all that uncommon for him to be camping and all of a sudden Aborigines would come into his camp, still wearing the old possum cloaks and carrying their spears and whatnot. So, like on Dad's side, on Mum's side there was a lot of fellow feeling for the blacks. I think Grandad Walter was a bit troubled knowing that all the land he was surveying inevitably meant the demise of the blacks' way of life. He was pretty much alone in that way of thought of course, because the settlers generally were too intent on their own survival to worry about these primitive blackfellows. Some of those settlers saw the blacks as just another hindrance to be got rid of. A bit like ringbarking.

If you look at a map of Kiandra, you'll see there's a gully not far from here called Black Walter's. I believe that's named due to one of Grandad's Aboriginal friends, who named his son after Walter after Grandad showed some kindness or other. I don't know the details but at that time when things were still hot on the frontier in some places, any kindness was pretty rare. Maybe Walter just gave them some tea or tobacco or something; I simply don't know now.

There's a few places around Kiandra named after people or incidents in my family history. I get a great sense of connection out of that. When I'm here in this little room in Tumut, all I have to do is get out the map and look at some of those names and I'm back there again.

But anyway, as I was saying, Walter came out here and he met a young German woman named Elsa. She was the daughter of German gold diggers from Bremen. They'd not done too well on the diggings down in Victoria. You know it was the Germans who named no-good mineshafts 'shicers'? Yeah, it came from their word for 'shit'! I hope that's not too rude for your interview, but that's the German contribution to the Australian vernacular.

Her folks moved up to New South Wales and became farm labourers and shearing cooks out west of the Darling. Huge properties out there and millions of sheep. So Elsa met Walter when he was out Wilcannia way surveying property boundaries. They lived in a tent for their first four years of marriage. Dust, flies, maggoty beef – you can imagine. And that's where Mum was born, on the hot plains west of the Darling.

They raised Edie as best they could and she got a job as a domestic help down at Delegate. Eventually she found her way to Kiandra and married Dad, Tom Leong. I don't think she ever went back to the flat lands. She loved it in the high country, and used to say she was born to be in the mountains, so it's lucky that she found them. Or maybe they found her. Her grave's there in the little Kiandra Cemetery on Permanent Creek. I've always loved the humour in that: Permanent Creek indeed – sure is, for those buried there!

11

Of course, while I said that this was my mum's family background, I know that my biological mother's story was totally different. But I'll never know what it was, because I'll never know who she was.

Did it worry me that I had been dumped on a doorstep by my birth mother? No, it didn't. Because Edie and Tom raised me with so much love, I hardly ever thought about who my 'real' mother was and it became an irrelevant question. Naturally, my story was something of a scandal for some in the town, especially at the time I was found in the soapbox in the blizzard. But as time went on, I was mostly accepted by the Kiandrans.

One thing I always noticed, though, was that often when I was walking down the street – and not just as a child but as a young adult when there were still lots of people around who remembered my presumably 'illegitimate' birth – I would get odd looks from various women. I realised quickly that they were trying to work out who I might resemble, and who the couple might have been who conceived me. The looks became more intense as I grew older and my features more pronounced. I have no doubt that a topic of conversation for decades in Kiandra, as those women gathered for their gossip sessions around pots of tea and scones, was who the naughty young woman and beastly man were who begat me.

I actually thought it was funny that my 'begatness' should so preoccupy some of the townsfolk, so I decided to have some fun with it. This was why I was constantly growing facial hair once I was old enough to do so, and changing it. I'd grow a beard, then shave off most and leave a moustache. Then I'd get rid of the lot and do vice versa. Likewise, I'd grow my hair long and then cut it short. Hopefully I was successful in frustrating the gossip mongers around town.

Actually, I never wanted to find out who my real parents were. Life as part of the Leong family was good enough for me, and judging by some of the other families around, I was pretty lucky to be where I was. Maybe that was why my birth mother had left me on Edie and Tom's doorstep – she knew that they could give me a much better life than she ever could. For that piece of wise insight, I thank her – whoever she was.

Mum never tolerated anyone speculating over the identity of my biological parents. As far as she was concerned, she and Tom were my parents and that was that. If she overheard some of the gossipers, she would walk right up to them and tell them what for, in no uncertain terms! She wasn't a big woman physically, but she had a huge heart. She always treated me just like her other kids, as did Tom.

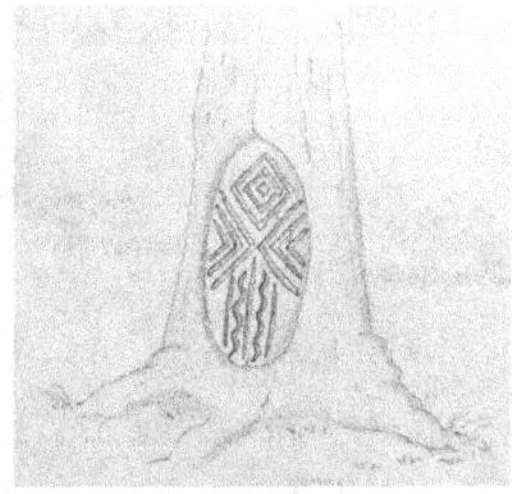

12

There were a few ways that we in the Leong family used to celebrate our mixed cultures. By the time I came along, the town's joss house was long gone, but some hangovers from the colourful Chinese past remained. Dad and a few of the other Chinese-Australians around the district would get together on some special Chinese day or other and set off fireworks. Some they made themselves, others they got from Sydney through Chinese importers. The sky rockets and crackers made a real spectacle and all the townspeople joined in the fun. Of course it was at night, and any night in Kiandra is a cold one, so there'd be a huge bonfire too. It was a much bigger event than Empire Day, when the rest of Australia had its fiery celebrations.

Those fireworks nights were wonderful, particularly for us kids, but as they say, all good things must come to an end. In this case, they came to a particularly fiery end. One year, maybe it was 1907 or something – it was before the Great War anyway – one of Dad's rockets didn't go off. So he picked it up to see what the problem was, when – whoosh – it shot out of his hands and straight across the street, smashing through a window into the back room of the Alpine Hotel. Within minutes, the window curtains were on fire and flames started licking the surrounding timber work! So, Dad and the other men grabbed buckets – we never had a fire brigade, which in a timber-built town was always a bit of a worry – and after a few heart-stopping minutes got things under control.

Old Ernie Weiss the publican was pretty annoyed about that, as you could imagine, and Dad had no choice but to put a stop to the fireworks from then on. Oh, we'd occasionally let a few off up at our place, but it was never anything like those big nights in town.

As for the German thread in the family blood, Mum used to make this sort of pork sausage, flavoured with lots of spice and pig's blood, and steamed for hours in the big pot over the fire. So it was rather like the black pudding of the English, but a bit stronger flavoured. She called it wurst, and how authentic it was I couldn't say but she always used it to remind us of those Bremen ancestors of ours. But to be honest, it probably was about as genuine as pickled pig's trotters. She also fermented sauerkraut (cabbages stored well through the Kiandra winter) and the smell while she warmed it for eating would waft off Poverty Hill and over the neighbours. Kiandrans knew when we were having our German nights! But the cabbage was a lot better than the smell of some of the locals' outhouses which we would cop in an easterly, that's for sure.

As for my Aboriginal heritage, I could say that at times we lived like Aborigines, but then so did much of the town. We'd shoot the odd wallaby or kangaroo and stew it or fry it. Mum made kangaroo tail soup many times. Dad would use the skins from those sorts of animals and possums too to make rugs. Roo and possum rugs were quite common amongst the bush people. Rabbit skins too. But we were not alone in all of that as many of our neighbours resorted to bush meat and skins – there was never a huge amount of cash around so people used their own resources as best they could. Dad would use rabbit traps at the base of trees to trap possums in order to save on the money he would have spent on bullets if he'd had to shoot them.

I guess the real times that our Aboriginal blood showed up was when blacks were passing through town. Occasionally Ngarigo, Wiradjuri, Wolgal or others would come through Kiandra on their way to visit family or their country elsewhere. The police would always get a bit blustery then and move those people on. Even if the blacks were camped way down near the Eucumbene, the coppers would force them on towards Adaminaby or the other way to Tumut. So, whenever Dad saw those people coming through, he'd offer them a bed for the night. He'd try to get to them before the police. In that respect, we were different to the rest of the townsfolk. It was rare indeed for anyone else to offer a roof to the blackfellas.

In time, I was to learn a lot more about who the Aborigines were, and what being an Aboriginal meant.

13

When I was a youngster, there was a very interesting group of Chinese miners still working up on the slopes over the back of Bullock Head Creek. They'd been in Kiandra for years, not since the original rush but from about 1870 when they'd moved here from old claims around Araluen. The thing was that by the time I was a boy, most of the Chinese who had come to the goldfields had either gone back home to China or had assimilated into the Australian community, growing market gardens, running stores and whatnot. They'd learnt some English, dressed in Australian clothes and changed their hairstyle. But this gang from Araluen never did assimilate. They kept the old cotton Chinese trousers and shirts, wore the Chinese-style hats, still wore pigtails, and mostly never learned English. Only their headman Su Bo Long could speak any English and it was pretty accented. So my father was their main contact in town, because he could speak Cantonese as well as Mandarin. Most of that group were middle-aged men by then, so they must have been tough to keep to the mining life with all its rigours and precious little rewards.

Chinese miners on the goldfields had a very distinctive way of working. When you sluice, there's lots of rocks in the soil that have to be removed. Many of the white digging parties used to just heave the stones out of the way, not really caring where they ended up. But the Chinese were much more methodical. They'd neatly stack the rocks into mounds with straight walls. The rocks were mostly water-worn and rounded by the ancient streams that the miners were excavating for the gold, so where there were Chinese miners you'd have all these neat, walled mounds of river rocks. These blokes on Bullock Head were like that, and you can still see their rock mounds there today.

Anyway, about 1905 or '06 (I forget the actual year but you could check it in the old copies of the Cooma newspaper), there was this very wet season. It was spring and the ground was already wet from the snowmelt, then with all this rain it was absolutely saturated. This Chinese group were just getting their hydraulic sluicing gear going again after the winter. They were keen to win some gold again, and have some money. They'd started up the monitor nozzle and were starting to sluice when this big landslip occurred. Tons of soil just slid down the hill above the creek, carrying trees and boulders and all, and landing right in the middle of the miners. Three of them instantly disappeared, buried in the mud. So the others frantically started digging for them.

It was hopeless, so Bo Long grabbed his bicycle (none of them owned horses) and rode into town to Dad's store. I and brother Jim happened to be there and I still remember Bo Long running into the store and yelling at Dad about an accident (Jim and I knew a bit of the lingo too). With that, Dad told us to jump onto his buggy while he spread the word among the other townspeople, and soon a cavalcade of horses, riders and vehicles was rattling along the track to the spot.

The Chinese miners were digging madly to get down to the three missing men. We joined in and Jim, Dad and I were on shovels. It must have been at least forty-five minutes or so since the slide by now, so time was of the essence if we were to save anyone. We were all digging down, mud flying everywhere, everyone in it together, no difference whether they were Chinese, Irish, English, Australian, German, American, whatever.

I always remember Dad calling out, 'Dig together, boys, dig together.' He was like the commander-in-chief. 'Dig together, boys.'

And we did.

After about ten minutes, Dad suddenly exclaimed and jerked upright. He'd uncovered a man's hand. Dad began pulling the mud away with his own hands and more of the man emerged. When he got to the chap's head, the Chinaman let out this huge gasp, spitting dirt everywhere and taking great gulps of air. He'd been trapped in an air pocket luckily for him, and so was still alive. Jim and I worked with Dad to free him. We then laid him out and some of his compatriots rushed over to tend him. He was in shock but it looked like he was going to live.

Then two of the Chinese found a second man. But he was blue and obviously dead. That was the first dead man I had ever seen. Mud was coming out of his mouth and his open eyes were bulging like a frog. It was a terrible thing.

Not long after, some of the blokes who Dad had dragged out of the bar at the Alpine Hotel found the third digger. He too was alive but with a badly broken arm. Gasping and crying, he was freed from the mud.

Doctor James had arrived by now and the pub blokes went to put the Chinaman in his buggy, but the doc would have none of it. He didn't want this muddy Chinese spoiling his buggy. 'Put him in the dray,' yelled Doc.

So the digger was laid in the dray and driven back to town and the surgery, with Dr James following in his clean buggy.

That was quite a day. Although one of the men died, two lived. What's more, the emergency saw the town come together in a way that made many feel proud. I know that Dad was very pleased that when the call was made for help, people responded, regardless of who the miners were. It was an event that mountain people talked of for years, the day that Kiandra did itself proud. No one ever mentioned Doc's concern about his buggy, though.

14

Kiandra's schoolhouse was a distinctive little building in the town. It was weatherboard like almost everything else but had a curved iron roof. I think that style was called beehive or something. The name was to do with the building shape, though this kid Duncan Donaldson used to have a funny accent and thought the name was because us kids never 'beehived' ourselves when we were there. Like most bush schools, there was only one teacher, who used to board with one of the families. I'm glad he never boarded with us. Imagine having to behave yourself twenty-four hours a day! Discipline in those days was pretty tough – few of us boys escaped the cane, and even some girls got a few cuts – so it was a relief to leave school each afternoon.

Some of the kids who lived further out rode horses to school and in the winter all of us would ski there, even those who lived only a few blocks away. In Kiandra, kids learned to ski almost as soon as they could walk. We'd often have races, especially on the way home, and in the spring when the snow was beginning to melt there would be big muddy puddles in the streets which we'd try to knock one another into if we could as we raced along. Many was the time I arrived home splattered with mud – much to Mum's annoyance.

But I gave as good as I got and one day I decided to get Spotty Finlayson. Spotty used to tease all the girls and on one occasion he'd dipped my sister Belle's ponytail in the inkwell. She had beautiful blonde hair (no doubt a Teutonic inheritance via Mother) and was very peeved. So I decided to deal with Spotty on the way home. I challenged him to a race, which he of course accepted. As we built up speed and were just about to go past the horse stables near the top pub, I shouldered him with all my might. He went straight over into the biggest puddle in the street and, what was best of all, the puddle was as much horse manure as it was mud! Spotty sat there for a few seconds looking dazed and most undignified. He was a sorry sight as he headed home, dripping, on his own. He never touched Belle's hair after that. I was Belle's hero.

Mind you, such sibling loyalty was often short-lived. One other time when Belle and I were fighting in the kitchen over which of us was going to go out with Dad rabbit-shooting, I grabbed a pair of Mum's scissors and in a rash moment cut off a hunk of Belle's hair. Frenzied, she then went for the carving fork and thrust it into the back of my neck. Blood spurted out and at first she thought she'd killed me. Of course, I milked it for all I was worth, living on sympathy for at least the next few hours. After all that, neither of us went shooting with dad; Mary went instead, as punishment to us.

I've still got that scar too; if I bend my neck, you can see it – see there?

15

One thing about my parents that I will always be thankful for was that when I was young they let me roam. Once I was old enough to ride a horse and not fall off too often, they just let me go. So long as I gave them some indication of where I was heading and when I'd be back, they were happy for me to have some adventures in the bush.

So, through my early years and teens, I rode about the place at will and that was why, when it came to that time a bit later when I had to take supplies out to outlying camps, I never had a problem navigating. I just knew the hills by then.

One of the most memorable of those early trips was when I stayed out all night. When I broached that one with Mum and Dad, Mum was a bit apprehensive but Dad said, 'Edie, let him go. It'll be good for him. Probably as educational as a day down at the school.' So Mum, slightly grudgingly, agreed and off I went.

On my horse of that time, Lord Byron (a classy name, which stemmed from Dad's interest in English poetry, and as he was part brumby perhaps he reflected the Lord's own reputed wildness), I rode out to the west on the ridges above the big drop-off to Lobbs Hole. The views out that way at sunset were absolutely stunning. I continued on until it was too dark to keep riding.

So I got off Lordy, as I called him, and just sat. I sat in the snowgrass in the snowgum forest for hours. The moon came up and cast a beautiful light, strong enough to make sharp shadows from the trees. After a while, boobook owls started calling. Crickets and other night-time insects chirped away. Then I heard a powerful owl make its distinctive call in taller timber down below. Wombats were out and feeding by now and I could hear their gruff calls and snorts as they dug up roots and bulldozed their way through the undergrowth. One came almost right up to me, snuffling and pawing at the ground. It looked towards me but didn't seem frightened, and just moved in a circle around where I sat. A light breeze might move through the leaves and the gentle murmur only heightened the magic of that night. And it was magical.

That night woke in me a little bit more of my appreciation of the bush. I was probably seeing and hearing things that most of the other kids at the Kiandra school never experienced. I treasured that night.

Anyway, come dawn, I made my way back home. After an hour or two, the town came into sight and the first smoke was rising from people's chimneys. When I was about a hundred yards from home, Dad came out the door, about to head to the store to open up for the day. I whistled to him and he turned and gave me a grin and a wave. That night I told him and Mum all that I had experienced. They could see how the experience had excited me. Good old Mum and Dad.

16

Having been born into a goldfield, I had all my early life shaped by that goldfield landscape. I grew up thinking that piles of rocks, deep gullies, large erosion pits and all the other marks left by miners was normal. But as I started to think about it all a bit further, and get to know the surviving natural world a bit more, I did start to question that.

When the miners were sluicing, the creeks and eventually the Eucumbene River into which they flowed, would turn grey. All the soil they were washing to get at the gold flowed down the tail races into the creeks and eventually ended up in the river. I had not really thought about that very much when I was a kid but as a teenager I started to get a bit anxious when the beautiful clear waters turned into this horrible soup. Sometimes you could almost stand a spoon upright in the water, it was that thick with sediment.

During my fishing trips along the creeks and the Eucumbene, I sometimes found dead fish, trout floating belly up. Then I found a dead platypus. Water rats also would turn up dead. That certainly didn't seem quite right. I knew people in town who hunted platypus and water rats for their skins – they could fetch good prices with skin buyers in Cooma and Queanbeyan. I never went in for that, as I felt those animals were a bit more special than the rabbits whose skins I and my siblings sold. So when I found them dead after a busy sluicing period, I started to reconsider just what we were doing to the wild world in our neck of the woods.

But as you'll see, it took me a long while to come to terms with that line of thought. My own need to earn a living had to come first, just like for everyone else. It would be many years before I could really confront the little accusatory finger that had started wagging at the far back of my mind.

17

I said earlier that, at the time I was born, the Leongs were in a slab hut. It was a pretty rough affair, and not what you'd think the town storekeeper would be living in. The thing was that old Grandfather Sam believed firmly that everyone should make it on their own. He was a tough old bugger and didn't give a helping hand to any of his sons, Dad included. But when Grandad finally passed away, there was a will and Tom, as the most industrious one in the family, got a helpful inheritance.

As a result, the house was rebuilt with weatherboards, and board ceilings unlike the old calico ones which the possums used to make holes in. The roof was new corrugated iron, instead of the rusty old second-hand stuff that was on the first house. Mum and Dad were both very proud of the new cottage. When Charles Kerry was in town for the ski races and taking his photographs, Dad got him to take some pictures of the house, with all of us standing outside. You can see that print in some of the library collections of Kerry's work. Kerry did a lot of good for Kiandra. Many people up in Sydney probably would never have heard of the town had it not been for him giving us some publicity and bringing down some tourists for the snow.

The ski races (always called snowshoe races in those early years) that the town held, and that brought Charles down here, also saw an incident that greatly damaged my first love affair. It was my only love affair really and, if I was honest about it, it was the deepest source of regret that I've ever experienced.

18

Despite that fact that us Leongs mixed in pretty well with the rest of the town, regardless of our background, I suppose it's not surprising that I sometimes gravitated to some of the other immigrants or their descendants. The Carluccios were the only Italians in Kiandra. When you think of Italians you think of swarthy types, heavily built sorts. But that's the southern Italians. Those from the north are very different, and that's where Ennio Carluccio and his wife Giuseppina came from. They had six kids (being good Catholics of course): three boys and three girls. They'd had more but, as was not uncommon in those days, they'd lost one or two at birth. Mrs Carluccio was never a well woman after those losses, but she always put on a brave face and battled on. Ennio knew English pretty well, but Mrs only really spoke Italian and a sort of halting English that got her to the shop and back.

Anyway, all the Carluccio kids were good-looking. (Of course it's hard for a bloke like me to say the boys were good-looking; if I'd said that too often, people would have got suspicious of me. But you know what I mean – they were handsome types in the way of so many Italians.) But it was the girls who were really striking and the pick of the bunch was Giulia. She was a pretty little girl and grew into an absolutely beautiful woman. Deep green eyes, long sandy-coloured hair, a faultless complexion and a slim figure with lovely curves.

Giulia and I were the same age and at school we sat near each other. She was more friendly than some of the other kids and from a young age we became friends. Some of the kids at Kiandra's school were real brats. You know, throwing screwed-up paper at other kids, shooting spitballs around, playing up whenever the teacher had his back turned. But Giulia was well behaved, and I tried to be well behaved too, I guess to impress her (also, if I'd played up, my siblings would have told on me, especially Mary, who was a real little tittle-tattle).

It's funny that one of my earliest memories of that school is eating my sandwiches with Giulia out in the playground one lunchtime. I say 'playground' but it was just clear land out the back, with a few boulders sticking up and a sluice gully from the earlier mining days.

As we got older, Giulia and I spent more time together. Not only boys liked to go fishing in the Eucumbene; girls did too. Trout had been introduced by then and casting a line was popular. Giulia would come by our place with her rod and call out to me, 'Are you coming down to the river?' Mum always let me go, and Dad loved fish so he encouraged me to bring back a bag full. It was during times like that, or a few years later when we'd ride our horses in the hills, that Giulia and I became close. She loved the bush (she'd not known anything else really) and when the wild flowers were out in the summertime, she and I would pick some when we stopped to spell the horses.

She'd been born in Australia but had a little bit of an accent from her parents. Whenever she saw me, she'd say, 'Hey, Leslie' with this cute sort of Italian twist to it, emphasising the syllables in my name really different to the way others said it. I really loved that!

As I grew up, I somehow learned about sexual relations. I don't recall Dad telling me about it but I guess that kids just learn these things. I remember one night at home when I had started to know about men and women, hearing from my parents' room Mum say to Dad, 'Turn over.' He turned, and Mum then said, 'No, the other way.' There then began murmurs and groans and whispers and I put the pillow over my head in embarrassment. I was now old enough to know what they were doing.

Before I was through my teens, I knew that I really wanted to have Giulia. But she had developed a bit quicker than me. Despite our close friendship and my feelings for her, she had started showing interest in other boys. Maybe I was too shy for her, or too slow. Also, as she got older, despite her love for the bush, she started wanting a bit more to her life. Maybe Kiandra wasn't enough for her and she wanted to know what was beyond. Anyway, when tourists came to town in the winter, she would always be wanting to chat to them, especially the young men. Although she and I had fun in the races, sometimes competing against one another, I started to get anxious about all the time she was spending with these Sydney blokes.

Of course, to many of those tourists we were just country hicks. Some of them really lorded it over us. But when it came to Giulia they were as smitten as any young man would be.

One night, in July 1912 (I'll never forget the date), after the ski club races, a few of us, locals and Sydney-ites alike, were having a drink at the pub in celebration. It was a convivial occasion, for despite some of the visitors' lordly attitudes, we were more or less on equal terms when it came to the racing. Giulia and some visiting young men and ladies were in the parlour at the back (no women in the bar, of course) and after a time I went in to see her. I was surprised to find that she'd left the room (normally we would have walked to our homes together). So I went out through the back door to head home, hoofing it through the slush and snow as usual. But as I rounded the corner of the stables I heard a weird sort of cry from inside. It reminded me a bit of that night at home and my parents' love-making. So I squeezed the door ajar. It was dim inside, with just a candle burning. But that was enough light for me to see what was happening. There was Giulia, lying back against some hay bales, her skirts up, with this bloke up against her. His pants were down – I'll never forget the sight of his white bum going in and out.

Well, I was completely astounded. I was embarrassed. I was angry. I didn't know what to do. Giulia's cries seemed on the one hand pained, on the other full of pleasure. I knew about rape – there had been a case recently in Cooma. Was that guy raping her? Or did she want him? I stepped quietly through the door and came up behind them. Giulia had her eyes closed and was moaning, crying out intermittently, and he was – well, all I can describe it as, was grunting. At that moment, Giulia opened her eyes and saw me. Her look was one of terror, and yet of pleading too. Pleading for me to help her, or to leave her alone? Was she embarrassed too, was that what she was trying to show in her eyes?

I was almost beside myself with emotions. Clear thought was impossible. In an instant, I picked up a nearby broken axe handle and brought it crashing down on the man's head. He collapsed and Giulia screamed at me.

'What are you doing, you fool?' she yelled.

I yelled back, 'I'm trying to help you.'

She slapped my face, pulled her skirts down and ran past me out of the barn in tears.

Luckily, what with the piano accordion music and singing in the pub, no one had heard our fracas. I was in a misty haze of heat and cold, of uncertainty where I just didn't know what was next. Obviously I had to get the bloke out of the stable and to try to bring him round. So I dragged him by the heels out and under the back veranda, threw some cold water over him, and when he started groaning I took off.

I didn't sleep that night.

Next morning, I went down to the pub and asked about that day's races. I knew the Sydney bloke was scheduled to compete. Charles Kerry said that their team was one short, owing to one of their members having too much to drink and passing out on the back veranda. I knew I'd had a lucky escape.

But Giulia didn't speak to me for weeks, and I didn't speak to her. I knew of course that she had wanted that man, rather than me. I was heartbroken to have apparently lost her friendship. All those shared experiences that we'd had over the years started to decay in my memory. The past became black. Whenever we passed in the street, she looked away. I thought it was because of what I'd done. But over time I realised that she was just as upset about what she'd done. She was intensely humiliated by being found out and by the randomness of her act, and I guess for a while she lived in fear that I'd start blurting about her around town and her reputation would be ruined. Just what her parents would have said and done defies thinking about. Of course I never wanted to hurt her. The secret was ours alone. By the grace of God, she didn't get pregnant. Gradually we started talking again. Perhaps there was still hope for us for the future?

19

Not long after, all our lives were turned upside down. The war broke out. I'll always remember Dad bringing home the newspaper with this black look on his face. Dad was an intelligent man and knew that war is never good. He was terribly concerned about what would happen. Many people around town jumped on the jingo bandwagon and beat the patriot drum, calling on us young men to enlist. But Dad and Mum (Mum with her German ancestry was nervous of the backlash) feared the catastrophe that might emerge. When the casualty lists started coming back from Gallipoli and then France, my parents were proved right.

Many young men from the mountains did join the army. Of course they were good on horseback, could shoot straight and were strong and used to roughing it. Just the sort of men for the Australian Imperial Force. But you only have to look at the war memorials built after the war ended to know how many of them didn't make it home.

But for me, the biggest impact was that I lost Giulia for four – no, nearly five – years. Two of her brothers, Genaro and Tom, enlisted. Giulia, high spirit that she was, wouldn't be left behind. She joined as a nurse. She'd had experience treating broken legs from horse falls and a few axe cuts, so I suppose the military grabbed that sort of woman. She certainly had a spark, and if anyone could handle the blood and guts of those casualty clearing stations and hospitals on the Western Front then she could.

Despite my parents' feelings against the war, I was tempted to enlist. That Giulia had gone was an added incentive and caused me much grief as I tried to weigh up my parents' feelings against my own. Snowy Gilbert, Jim Bradley, Vince Oldfellow were friends who went into khaki. Their talk of adventure almost overcame Mum and Dad's words about death and waste and politics. But I did my duty to my parents, and stayed home. Perhaps in that way I was still doing my duty to my country too – as I found out, someone had to keep things going on the home front.

Soon, with men going away, there were too few to keep all the little mining operations and grazing leases going. So, for the ones who did continue, I was a bit of a godsend, because I could work for them. Since leaving school, I'd become pretty good on horseback and could ride for days without bother. Soon I had the job of taking supplies by packhorse out into the hills to resupply the miners and the stockmen in their little huts and camps.

During those times, I got to know the mountains like the proverbial back of my hand. Knowing the country out in the western plains is easy. I know that Banjo Paterson wrote about Clancy of the Overflow as if he was a hero, but Clancy had it easy out on the plains. It was the mountain country that was the real challenge on horseback. Banjo did get it right there, with his Man from Snowy River (and there's a few riders who I've known who might have inspired Banjo to write that poem, don't you worry). We were all proud of our ability to get around even the roughest country, either taking stock through, or leading packhorses like I did so many times. Banjo skied a few times at Kiandra with Kerry and the others from Sydney. I recall he was a lawyer and he certainly looked the part, all done up with fresh shirt collar and quality waistcoat and all. Most of us wore oilskins outdoors, but Banjo had tweed. He was a city man, that's for sure, but he did listen to our stories with intensity around the pub bar. I know he was born on a station and maybe those early days left him with a link to the bush.

Some of those little camps that I rode out to were very primitive affairs. Just a simple hut with an open fire and the camp oven sitting by the coals and a billy hanging on a wire above. Out the back there'd usually be a pile of rum and beer bottles, empty sardine tins and what have you. Bed might be a sapling frame with a sheet of hessian stretched across it instead of a mattress, a few blankets on top – sheets were a luxury. They'd have a canvas or metal water bucket that they'd take to the creek – that's the real beauty of the mountains, there's just about always good fresh water nearby.

Half those blokes lived on possum and wallaby, but they'd order salt meat and flour and a few pounds of spuds. There'd be tea and sugar too of course, and tins of golden syrup, and other tinned things. Maybe powdered milk. That's where I came in, packing the supplies from Dad's store out to the camps.

I'd always know when I was getting near a camp because you'd smell the woodsmoke drifting up from their fireplace. The billy was always on and those blokes'd offer me a cup of tea and a bit of damper. I was one of the few people they'd see so they always wanted to chat, sometimes for an hour or more.

I'd be interested in how their prospecting was going, but they were always pretty cagey about how they were doing. 'Making rations' was the common reply – in other words, not getting much. Well, more than a few of them were rumoured to have a pickle bottle of nuggets stashed somewhere around or under the hut. Often when blokes died, others would make a beeline for their hut and have a snoop around. I don't think the under-bed El Dorado was ever found, though! All those men had one thing in common. Whenever they talked about gold, they'd get this weird gleam in their eye, like they were somewhere else. Gold can breed a kind of madness and I'd say many of those blokes suffered from it.

But they did open up about other things, and what I learned from some of those men you wouldn't believe now. 'Black' Harry Thompson (he was named Black to distinguish him from all the other Harrys in the Thompson family) had served in the Boer War. Australia was all very proud of what its men had done in South Africa and many towns built their war memorial to those who didn't return. But Harry had a different view. He told me about the concentration camps where the Brits – and Aussies – put the Boer civilians and their families. They were basically prisoner-of-war camps. The Boers starved there, and Harry spoke in low tones about women and children just skin and bone, wearing little more than rags. Yards full of walking skeletons.

Harry said the Boer fighters were farmers, not so different to many of our blokes who went over to fight them. He felt pretty uneasy about doing Britain's bidding against rural people like that. He wondered what gave him the right to kill people so similar to himself. That's why he went bush when he came back. As for the Great War, he didn't want to know about it.

Many of the lone men out in the mountains were like Black Harry. You know, a bit damaged sort of thing. Fred Hansen had lived in Sydney. He ran a clothing business in George Street, right in the centre of town. But one night he ran into a mob from The Rocks. You know, part of the Push. They had pick handles and what not and demanded Fred hand over his wallet. He was a proud man Fred and he told them to piss off. Well, that was it. They got stuck into him and left him for dead with broken cheek bones, a fractured arm, and no wallet. After that, he never really recovered, so like Harry he took to the bush.

I think it was Henry Lawson who likened the bush to a sort of sanatorium for wounded minds. He hit the nail on the head there.

Tommy Fishbourne was aged about ninety when I knew him, living in a hut near Milk Shanty Creek. Amazing that someone so old could still be living on their own in the bush. He was a bit like old Sailor. Tommy had come out as a convict back around the late 1830s, just in his teens. When he'd served his time, he followed the gold and went down to the Victorian fields, Mt Alexander, Bendigo, Beechworth. He met Alfred Howitt and they became friends. When the government appointed Howitt to go in search of the explorers Burke and Wills back in about 1861, Tommy was part of his team. They found Burke and Wills, dead, out near Cooper Creek. One of the bodies had been partly eaten by dingoes by then.

Anyway, Tommy and the others gave them a decent burial. They found King, the only survivor, and he was living with the blacks, the Yandruwandha. It was only the blacks that had saved him. They knew how to catch fish in the creek and get ducks and they ground up this nardoo seed and made flour for johnny cake sort of things. The Aborigines there, like everywhere else, knew how to live in this land, but the whitefellows didn't and some didn't live long enough to learn how. After that, Tommy worked on some of the desert goldfields around Tibooburra, where there was no water and they had this thing called a 'dry blower', using wind to separate the gold from the soil. Tommy got jack of that and ended up here in Kiandra, where there's plenty of water and its nice and cold. He'd had enough heat, dust and flies for one lifetime.

Probably the most shocking thing I ever experienced at that time was when I arrived at Vince Gollings's hut out at the Four Mile. Vince had been around for years, doing some mining and a bit of stock work. I noticed that as I approached his hut there was no smoke, which was unusual. I knocked on the wooden door but there was no answer. I did notice this strange smell, sort of sweet yet bitter too. A bit like burnt meat but not quite. Anyway, I squeezed open the door and walked in. Well, I couldn't believe what I saw. Vince had evidently fallen over, maybe in a fit of the DTs – he used to drink terribly like some of them up there. But he'd fallen into the fireplace, and his head was completely burnt away. God, what a sight. It was awful. I dry-retched and staggered outside. It took me a few moments to sort myself before I could ride back to Kiandra and tell the police. They duly went up and recovered the body. They brought Vince (or what was left of him) back wrapped in one of his old blankets and strapped lengthways to a packhorse. It was a sad little cavalcade that made its way into town. The townspeople passed the hat around to pay for his funeral, though the timber cross at the grave over at Permanent Creek has long gone. His hut's gone too of course, so you'd hardly know he'd ever existed. These people only really live on now in stories. Stories like mine.

One of the miners who particularly stands out in memory was Wilfred Henson. Wilf was about fifty-five when I used to take him his supplies. He had snowy-white hair and the bluest of blue eyes. When you were speaking to him and looking into those eyes it was like you weren't talking to a middle-aged man at all, but to a boy. He also had this ready boyish smile which sat well with the blue eyes. Wilf was different to the other diggers because he had no hesitation telling me how his prospecting was going. I guess he trusted me. If he had found a nugget, he would show me and I think it gave him pleasure to share his good fortune – when it occurred – with someone. One day he got out a particularly nice piece, about the size of my thumb. It was a beauty and one of the biggest nuggets I had seen.

Many of the other miners stayed on the goldfield until they were carried off in a box, but Wilf got out while the going was good. He bought a half share in a pub down in the Riverina at Darlington Point. The last thing I heard he was enjoying catching Murray cod when he wasn't behind the bar.

It was rare indeed for women to live out in the hills on their own, but one did. Marge Callahan was her name. Rumour had it she had been a madam at a Melbourne brothel (she called herself Marguerita), and had operated for years until the corrupt police that had been in her pay were dismissed and the commissioner cracked down on all these establishments in Fitzroy. Marge was certainly a fun woman, larger than life. She'd always invite me in and offer a rum, but I'd settle for tea.

Marge didn't seem to work; maybe she still had savings from all the night work. But she did have this fantastic collection of books which were her main form of company. Novels, poetry, philosophy, you name it, she was very well read. She was always reading when I arrived, when she wasn't tending her veg patch or rounding up her cow and calf for a bit of milk. Most winters she'd go off to Tumut to stay with relatives, but once the snow melted in spring, back she came. Funny thing, you'd think someone like that would be pretty foul-mouthed, but Marge always spoke with an educated accent. You could still see the beauty that she obviously was in her youth. She would have been popular in old Melbourne.

Marge is long gone now. I remember when she went off to Sydney when the bush life got just too hard. She just walked out of the hut and left all the books there. It was like this walk-in library, just sitting there in the bush. I borrowed some volumes, and returned them. But all the books eventually disappeared. I think many of the bush blokes simply used them for paper for the campfire, or other uses. Bit of a tragedy really.

Some of those loners really did sink into depravity. They'd been far too long on their own. The police used to have a charge called 'unnatural acts' or something like that. Well, there were one or two old bushies who were brought up on that charge at the Kiandra court. You know, they'd get caught with a sheep or a goat or something. I once saw that sort of thing happen. It was the end of a long day and I had one more hut to call into before heading home. It was John B's place (I don't think I should give his full name). I arrived and could hear this calf bellowing from behind his hut. So I dismounted and walked around the hut. Here was John, well and truly mounted, if you know what I mean. That was almost as much a shock as finding Vince Gollings's headless body.

But that sort of thing was pretty rare. In fact, what was surprising was that there weren't more weird goings-on. People who live mostly on their own really do stand a strong chance of going round the bend. Yet most of the men I knew out in the ranges looked after themselves. Yes, there was the pile of empty booze bottles behind almost every hut, and many of those characters were a bit fey, but somehow they held onto their sanity as best they could. If they had a white shirt, it was clean, and although one or two blokes were on the nose, the others kept themselves in pretty good shape.

20

It was around the time of the war that the first motor vehicle came through town. Yes, I seem to recall it was 1915, and the car was a Model T Ford. We'd heard about cars but most of the townsfolk had still not seen one. So when this Ford chugged and banged its way into town, there was considerable interest, to put it mildly.

The driver I think was a surveyor chap who had something to do with the federal capital. The government had decided on the capital site by then and although Dalgety had been an earlier choice, it was now Canberra. I don't know why the surveyor was over here in Kiandra; maybe he was involved with surveying the federal territory border. You can see some of the peaks on that border from around here, Mt Bimberi and others, so maybe that was it. Anyway, he had come through from Cooma, and the bush telegraph was hard at work and most of the town knew he was on his way even before he reached Adaminaby.

Many of the younger fellers in town (those who hadn't enlisted, that is) were pretty sceptical about this horseless carriage thing and thought it would be a good joke to see the driver try to get his jalopy through the Eucumbene River down the hill there. There was no bridge then, not like there is now. So they all rode out there on their horses, waiting to have a bit of a giggle at the city surveyor's expense. Many of the older folk too were unconvinced about motor cars at that time, but they were a bit more sensible and waited until the car made it into town. If it got through the river, then maybe it really was something worth looking at. The river crossing had for years been a bugbear for Kiandra folk. If the Eucumbene was in flood, then the coaches would have to stop till it went down, and in winter it was a real trial to get through.

After the car left Adaminaby, the postmistress there sent a wire through to our post office that the Ford was on its way. Before too long, the car came down the long slope from Sawyers Hill toward the river. This mud-spattered black metal vehicle with glass windshield and a leather top. Pretty noisy it was — you could hear it for miles. Down it came to the crossing and the young blokes on their horses were there waiting. The driver stopped, left the engine running and had a look at the ford. Then he got back in and revved her up and went in. The wheels went up over river stones and down the other side, splashing through the water, spinning in a bit of gravel here and there. But before long he was through. The blokes on their horses were a bit disappointed by that. And now they had to ride behind the chap, looking a bit sheepish.

The car came on up the long hill from the river and by the time it reached town there was quite a procession to welcome it. Kids were running alongside, riders were trotting too, and Dad and us kids came out of the store to have a look. Most of the town was there by this time. The car backfired once or twice and almost set off all the horses tethered in the main street. The surveyor chap then got out and asked Dad if he sold petrol. Of course he didn't, as at that time I don't think even a businessman as canny as Tom Leong had foreseen the coming of the car age and what it might mean for business. So Dad said no and the driver got one of his own cans of fuel that he had strapped to the running board and poured it into the tank. In those early days, petrol was very scarce outside towns and drivers had to carry substantial supplies. But straight away Dad could see a new branch of business. In no time, he started stocking fuel (in tins; a petrol pump came much later), oil, fan belts, spare parts and all the other paraphernalia that he could sell to passing motorists. It really was the dawn of a new age, and Dad was right onto it.

Having filled his tank, the surveyor got back in, restarted the car, and drove on his way toward Tumut. When he arrived in Kiandra, he was treated with scepticism, and when he left he was virtually a hero. I don't think there were many men (and not many women either) who that day didn't start thinking about buying their own car. Of course, cars were then so expensive that few of Kiandra's townsfolk could have afforded to purchase one. But such are dreams, and so is progress made.

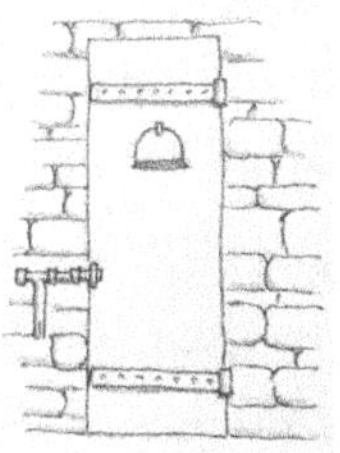

21

One other job I had in the war years was down at the police station. At that time it was run by Sergeant Cook and Constable Hutchison. There were two cells and from time to time there'd be a prisoner or two, who usually were locked up for a few weeks until the magistrate came by doing his rounds on the circuit court. Sergeant Cook gave me the job of mopping out the cells every week. Not much of a job but it was a little more cash. It had some other attractions too.

The prisoners would be out in the adjacent exercise yard when I was mopping out in the cells, and there were small barred windows between the cells and the yard, high up in the wall. So it was easy to hear what the prisoners were saying. I think they were always a bit fearful of the sergeant, but not so Hutch, as we used to call Cec Hutchison. The cons would refer to him by his rank, putting special emphasis on the first syllable of constable. It sounded very rude the way they said it, but I couldn't resist a giggle.

Two cons that I recall were especially memorable. Their names were Dunphy and Gillies and they were a pair of itinerant photographers who'd defrauded someone down around Wagga and been caught passing through town. So they were smart sorts of guys. They used to do this 'Cunst' thing at the top of their voice when Hutch was within hearing but I noticed once that Gillies had a black eye and Hutch a bandaged hand so perhaps the constable got his revenge.

The particular thing that these two men used to do was tell ribald jokes and play word games. They knew when I was in the cells because they could hear me slopping around, through the window, just as I could hear them. I think that sometimes they talked as much for my benefit as for theirs. They had a bit of a thing against the Catholic Church and most of their jokes were about a priest and four nuns, or a nun and four priests, or the Pope and various animals, that sort of thing. Maybe they'd had a hard time at a Catholic school somewhere. Mum and Dad were pretty strait-laced at home so these jokes were all new to me. At first I was rather scandalised but soon saw the humour.

Dunphy and Gillies played these word games too where one of them would say a word and the other had to match it with a rhyme. They'd go for as long as they could before one would submit defeat with 'Dunno'. One went something like

> It was fine
> To often dine
> After nine
> And drink the vine
> Oh so sublime
> When noses shine
> Not like mine
> For that I pine
> Now walk the line
> Dunno

I think they did one specially for me, because they knew who my father was and started this one with 'Rice'. At first I thought that was a bit racist but after a while I saw they were basically as much good-humoured and, frankly, bored, as much as they might have been mean-spirited. It went,

> Here's Rice
> Mopping mice
> And our lice
> And our vice
> In a trice

He's very nice
What's his price
For a dice
Or cocktail ice
Dunno.

If we passed when they were returning to the cells, they'd give me a wink, as if we were co-conspirators, or maybe they just appreciated the mopped-out cell.

Eventually their case was heard by Magistrate Mr Justice Berry and I think they were sentenced to something like two years in Cooma Gaol. For years, I wondered how they got on after that, whether they ever got back on the straight and narrow. Well, I found out, as I'll tell you in due course.

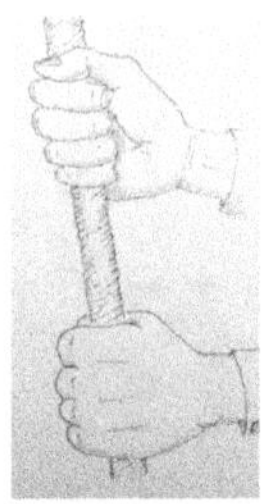

22

It was the year after the war that was one of the coldest that I'd ever known. The snow was deep, the ski races went particularly well, and we did a few ski trips cross-country to explore places we'd not seen much of in winter before.

But most importantly for me, Giulia returned. She'd written me occasional letters during the war, but only when she got back did I learn what the war had been like. It seemed unbelievable that civilised nations could wage a war like that, what with artillery, machine guns and that terrible mustard gas. We knew of course about the numbers who died, but Giulia's eye witness accounts really brought home to me just how barbaric humans can be. The Somme was a slaughterhouse from beginning to end. I'll always remember her description of a single shell exploding on a platoon of men and how none of them were left in recognisable form. Bits everywhere. How she endured all that, seeing so many young men die of terrible wounds and of infections, trying to ease those soldiers' last moments, coping with the mud and everything else. She was an amazing woman.

Back at home, Kiandra for her must have seemed like heaven. Giulia was certainly keen to make the most of that 1919 winter. So one day when the sun was out and the snow was deep and the air cold, we decided to ski to Three Mile Dam. The dam had been built by gold miners back about ten years before I was born to supply water to their hydraulic sluicing claims further down stream. In winter, the dam froze over and if the ice was thick enough, with a bit of powder snow on top, it could be a nice ski. But of course there was always a risk that the ice might be thin in one spot and you'd fall through.

By now I'd been taking tourists skiing for a few years. I'd show them some basic ski technique and we'd try the downhill runs above the town and sometimes go out into the bush for a bit of a tour sort of thing. I'd carry a pack with a few chops and a billy and we'd have a nice little barbecue and a cup of tea among the snowgums. It was a good little earner. On this trip with Giulia, two Sydney skiers joined us, Eric Nagle and Seb Francis. Eric and Seb had been to Kiandra before so I knew they could handle a longish trip.

Well, we did the long climb out of town heading west and then crossed the creek and headed up towards the dam. As I said, the day had started well with blue sky, but of course one thing the high country is famous (infamous?) for is changing weather. Sure enough, the westerly wind started to come up and so did the cloud. Soon there was a bit of snow flying past us but we kept going.

By the time we got to the dam, the weather was thick. Low cloud, strong wind and snow falling heavily. I asked Giulia, Eric and Seb if they were happy to go on and they said yes. They were determined to have a good time, and I was happy to take them. It was a nice opportunity to be with Giulia on her own or at least away from her family, so we could talk a bit.

We set out across the iced-up dam, me in front, then Giulia, then Eric, and Seb on the end. It was difficult to see the trees on the other side of the dam by this stage but I had a good sense of direction and had no qualms about getting lost. One thing I was concerned by, though, was a few cracks in the ice. I'd thought that, with the good snowfalls and cold temperatures, the ice would be fine, but it wasn't. I still can't think of an explanation for why the cracks were there on that day.

Anyway, we were by now right out in the middle. Suddenly there was this loud crack and behind me I heard Giulia and Eric both shout out in alarm. I turned just in time to see both of them falling through breaking ice into the frigid water. Seb luckily stopped in time, otherwise he would have fallen in as well. I quickly skied back the few yards to the hole and tried to calm Giulia and Eric, who were thrashing around in the water, unable to get out because the ice kept breaking around the edge. I yelled at them to kick their skis off underwater (bindings in those days were simple leather affairs), which they did, but they couldn't get a grip onto solid ice and I couldn't get close enough to them to grab their hands.

Things were rapidly getting desperate. I knew that I had to get them out otherwise they'd very soon lose consciousness in the freezing water. I then remembered that in my pack I had a length of light rope that I used occasionally for stringing up a tent fly at lunchtime when we had windy days on the snow and needed some shelter. I quickly got that out and threw the end of it to Giulia. The wind was that strong by now that I could barely make myself heard, but Giulia grabbed the rope and I started to haul her in. Miraculously, I was able to get her out onto the ice. Of course, she was soaked and now exposed to the wind as well, but Eric was still in the water. Snow was flying past so thickly that I could hardly see Eric but Seb shouted that he thought Eric was still treading water. I yelled to Eric and threw the rope again. The rope remained slack. I pulled it in and threw again. Still no sign of Eric having grabbed it. Seb now said he couldn't see Eric in the water. A momentary patch of clear air in the blizzard revealed that Eric was nowhere in sight. He'd gone under.

We couldn't do anything further for Eric. It would have been madness for either me or Seb to jump in to seek Eric under the surface, and Giulia by now was a shivering wreck, her clothes freezing to the ice. I got a spare oilskin jacket from my pack and wrapped it around her and forced her to her feet so I could carry her on over the frozen lake. Have you ever tried to carry someone when you're on skis? It's appallingly difficult. But anyway, somehow we got over into the shelter of the trees. Luckily, Seb was pretty fit and able to keep up. I knew there was a hut about a mile further on and I asked Seb to go ahead and find the hut and see if its owner, Bull McPherson, was there and to have the fire going when I arrived with Giulia.

I'll never forget that last mile. It was shocking. The weather continued to worsen. Although it was midday, it seemed like midnight. The wind shrieked like the banshees. Snowgum branches were snapping off around us. Cries of windblown crows came to us through the forest like the shrieks of witches. Bullets of snow and ice peppered our faces.

The first glimpse of the hut was a tremendous relief. There was Seb with Bull, and the fire was going. I got Giulia inside and changed her clothes for some old things Bull had. He was a huge man who didn't often wash his clothes but what he had was better than the finest fashions of Paris as far as I was concerned. Gradually, Giulia came round. I fed her a little warm tea, not too much at first.

She was at last able to talk. 'You didn't think you'd get rid of me that easily, did you?' she joked.

I could have cried with relief.

That night, we stayed at Bull's hut, sharing stew and some whisky that he had. The atmosphere, though one of relief over Giulia, was very sad on account of having lost Eric. Knowing that he was out there in the frozen lake recurred in nightmares during the night, when I woke up repeatedly, haunted by a drowning man's screams and an image coming at me from the green depths of a skeletal face intent on vengeance.

Morning finally broke and the dawn was beautifully calm and clear. We made our weary way back to Kiandra and to the police station to report Eric's death. A search party later had no luck on recovering the body. So Three Mile Dam remains Eric Nagle's memorial. The coroner visited Kiandra to hold an inquest which, though difficult in forcing the three of us to relive the experience, was nowhere near as harrowing as the real event itself. 'Death by misadventure' was the verdict. The experience left its mark on me and I never skied Three Mile Dam again.

The other impact of that day was that Giulia's health suffered. She had respiratory ailments for the rest of the winter. The doctor in town said she'd only recover if she got away to a warmer climate. So, accompanied by her father, she departed for Sydney to stay, indefinitely, with an aunt and uncle. Once again, we were to be separated. A lingering sense of guilt – not necessarily deserved or rational – stayed with me.

If Dad's inherited Chinese belief that luck was all around us, perhaps to the point of being some sort of entity, then Lady Luck had come halfway with me that day in saving Giulia, but had slipped away like a will-o'-the-wisp in the blizzards when it came to Eric.

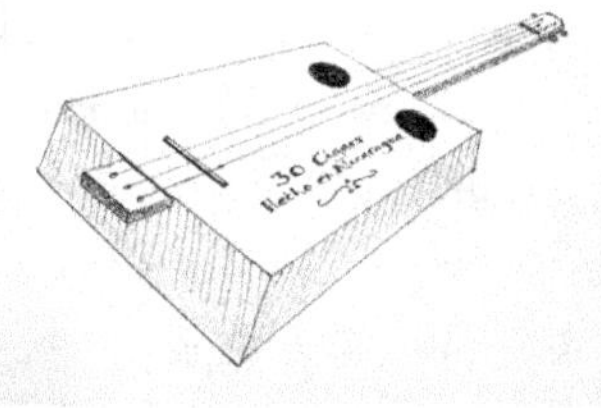

23

By now I was in my late twenties. We didn't really have big birthday celebrations at home. A few years earlier, I'd had my twenty-first birthday. Mum and Dad celebrated with me and my siblings with a huge chocolate cake that Mum made. Chocolate was a bit rare in our home, so it was special. I think back now about how fancy many people's twenty-firsts are and how modest mine was by comparison. But I had a good family and it was a happy evening.

If twenty-one represents a coming of age, a getting of wisdom, then I think I'd been getting wisdom over many years and now as I approached the end of my third decade I had a most unusual experience. I've mentioned how Aboriginal people occasionally passed through Kiandra and that Dad showed them kindnesses. Around this time, an Aboriginal man named Bruce Williams came to our home. It turned out we were actually related. Bruce was revered among his Ngarigo kin for his knowledge of the old ways. Dad thought it would be a good idea if I spent some time with Bruce, as with the end of the war and the return of some of the locals who had gone away, there was less work around the area. Bruce was heading down the coast to rejoin his family and the clan and was happy to take me with him. Not only could I help around their community at Lake Wonga, but Bruce led a gumleaf band which played at local events, and as I'd been learning the mouth organ maybe I'd get in on the musical act as well.

Bruce, Dad and I rode out to Adaminaby, from where Bruce and I got a lift in the mail car to Cooma and Dad took the horses home.

Dad wasn't getting any younger but he could still handle horses pretty well, so he was happy to help – it was his idea that I go with Bruce, after all. From Cooma, we caught one of the Balmain Brothers buses down through Nimmitabel and Brown Mountain to the far south coast. This was probably my first ride in a bus and it was rather exciting – what a country bumpkin I was! We arrived at Bega and then hitch-hiked to Lake Wonga. There were still not many cars then and when I say we hitched I mean on a dray, and it was a slow ride, but welcome. At the Lake, Bruce – and me by association – were greeted like returning, well-loved celebrities. The sense of community and family was palpable from the first moment.

I knew that many Aboriginal people had ended up on missions. Basically they'd been rounded up by the government and given little option but to go to these places, run by either government officials or churches. But Lake Wonga wasn't one of these. It was land of the coastal Yuin people and I think the Ngarigo community there were accepted in by the Yuin and simply built their houses on vacant land and settled down as neighbours of the Yuin. It wasn't the Ngarigo traditional mountain country, but at least they had some land, and certainly freedom. They were their own masters, much as they would have been in the old times before the coming of the settlers, my European and Chinese forebears included.

Once I was introduced and the Wonga people knew that I had some 'inherited' or 'adopted' black ancestry (Bruce made a point of that), I was made to feel very much at home. I soon had a big network of 'aunties' and 'uncles' that I'd never had before.

The houses were pretty ramshackle so I pitched in with the men to do a bit of home maintenance, and we built new houses when new families showed up. The flow of people was pretty fluid, so there were comings and goings all the time. Supplies came from Narooma, Cobargo or Bega. Some of the shopkeepers there had no worries about extending credit to the community, but others wouldn't even let blacks into their shops. So sometimes I went in and with my looks got through the more racist blockades.

There were quite a few Aboriginal people from the Yuin and other nations along the south coast so the Wonga clan was not alone. White community attitudes varied. Like the storekeepers, there were townspeople who were friendly and others that wouldn't allow blacks on their properties, and there were youths who'd shout out at you if you were trying to hitch a ride on the highway. I felt like a bit of a chameleon, sort of Aboriginal and sort of not, depending on where I was and who I was with.

But a point of connection between whites and blacks on the south coast was music. The Wonga gumleaf band, though not the only one on the coast at that time, was even then quite an institution. Their talent for playing this funny little instrument was considerable and they could adapt many of the hits of the time. They'd play these gumleaf tunes at the beginning and end of a show, and the rest of the time they played conventional dance band instruments. Bruce sang and played guitar. Jimmy was a very good drummer, Max was on saxophone, Arthur Pinkerton was on double bass, and Audrey played piano accordion. Places like Murrah Hall south of Bermagui really swung on Saturday nights. My harmonica skills developed under Bruce's tuition and soon I was playing with the band. The locals liked country and western, but the band always tried to stretch them a bit with some jazz and blues. Being Aboriginal, the band knew all about the blues. When playing jazz, and some of their blues too, they'd often do this thing they called syncopation, which I would have called offbeat, but whichever way you defined it, when we did it the locals all crowded the floor.

Bruce's acoustic guitar was made somewhere in Queensland from the lovely timber that they have up that way. He also had made for himself this little thing he called a cigar-box guitar. The sound box was, literally, a cigar box. Bruce explained to me that they were invented by poor musicians in the southern United States and they were common in blues circles. It seemed an appropriate instrument for Aborigines to be playing in southern NSW. Perhaps surprisingly, despite its humble construction and only having three strings, it had a nice sound. I never asked Bruce where he got the cigar box from. I knew he couldn't afford cigars.

I enjoyed the dances and got to know a number of local women. The girls at those dances were mostly dairy farmers' daughters. Big smiles, long plaits and flowing skirts that they'd swirl while they were dancing. And with all the farm work, they were fit and could really dance well, for hours on end. Blokes used to joke that with all the experience those girls had pulling cows' teats at milking time they'd be pretty good at other things too. They were an attractive lot, that's for sure, and I must say I was sorely tempted more than once. But apart from a simple kiss or two, and maybe a bit of a cuddle out the back of the hall, I stayed loyal to Giulia. I always wished that Giulia was there with me. Her occasional letters weren't much compensation for her absence.

As usual with bush dances, the blokes would be disappearing outside every now and then for a sip from a bottle. Dances were officially 'dry' but most blokes stashed a bottle behind a tree or somewhere. As the night went on, some of them would get the worse for wear and some of those who missed out on getting a girl to dance got snaky and inevitably there were fights. I don't think I've ever been to a bush dance where there wasn't a fight. Those coast blokes would really get stuck into it, especially the timber-cutters from the forests down there. I saw a few fellows end up black and blue and missing a tooth or two. They'd look as crook as Rookwood the morning after. For some of them it was sport – 'sooner have a fight than a f--k' as the old expression went (please excuse the crudity). But I always steered clear of that sort of thing. That night in the stable in Kiandra was the only time I've ever assaulted anyone and I wish I hadn't done it, but such is life sometimes, you know, passion and all. Hopefully that Sydney mate of Charles Kerry's wasn't too worse for wear when his headache wore off.

Probably the biggest thing that I learned from those couple of years, on and off, down at Wonga, was about the land and its spirit. Up at Kiandra I'd taken the land and the mountains, the trees, the snow and the animals a bit for granted. Of course, I liked it and felt close to it. But apart from the fledgling considerations about nature that I've already described, I hadn't thought much more deeply than that. Any sort of 'spiritual' connection was something I'd not considered, well not consciously anyway. Wonga changed all that, and I'm glad that it did.

Bruce and other senior men in the community, Ngarigo and Yuin, let me into some of their old stories. You would have heard of the Dreamtime. They explained to me their Dreamtime and its stories, of how creator beings made features in the landscape – this mound of rocks, that river valley, that peak on the Great Dividing Range, or that headland and the island just off it. The spirits of those creators were still part of the land, still with the people, and that gave those people a very strong connection that I was very impressed by.

When out in the forest with Bruce and the others, they'd point out these sorts of places and tell me ancient stories about animals too, like the koalas that even then were fast disappearing, or echidnas, snakes, lizards, eagles and of course the old kangaroo and swamp wallaby. The men could track animals and see birds in a way that was, well, just phenomenal. I thought I was pretty good in the bush, pretty observant, but they put me in the shade. They also knew all the plants, what could be used for medicine, what could be eaten, and what could be burnt at particular times of the year. Up in the snow leases around Kiandra, the graziers just used to burn at will in the autumn, to bring on green pick for the sheep next season. But the blacks had burning down to a fine art, and it really is an art, especially here in Australia where fire once started can become an absolute monster. Fire had been their tool for thousands of years. They'd hunted with it, cleared country with it, used it for ceremony of all sorts. No wonder they knew fire so intimately. I came to look at the land with new eyes and started to feel that stronger connection that the Wonga clan had.

There were secret places that Bruce wouldn't take me, places to do with the Yuin ancient initiation rites. I didn't mind that; after all,

I was only a visitor, and Bruce couldn't have gone there either as he was Ngarigo. But he did show me some rock carvings way up near the Divide and a very old painting of hands on the rocks there. I suddenly felt that I was surrounded by the spirits of these people, and that spirit – something that I'd never really thought about much before – was a very real thing. The church services that I'd occasionally attended as a boy at Kiandra had their own spiritual message which I'd not taken very seriously. But now I was looking anew. I was seeing spirit in land. Those times with Bruce gave me a respect for blacks and their ways that has stayed with me ever since. Sure, I'd always known that I had inherited Aboriginal connections, but now those connections were that much more real.

I must also say that not everything at Wonga impressed me. Like at Kiandra, alcohol was available, despite the legal ban for Aborigines. Somehow despite the laws then, grog was spirited into the community. Not everyone at Wonga drank, of course, but quite a few of the people did, particularly the men. And when drunk, some of the men used to beat their wives something terrible. You should have seen the scars. There was talk about banning drink in the settlement, but at the time I left, those moves had not progressed. There were also times when the tribal wars of old would erupt, and some of the Yuin blokes would attack the Ngarigo blokes, and vice versa. I could never work out just what triggered those fights, but they were doozies. The community had a lot going for it, but it wasn't a paradise.

24

I now had a way of looking at things that was pretty different to that of many of my friends up in the mountains. They regarded the Aboriginal ways as simple superstition. So I learned to keep my mouth shut rather than face ridicule. But it was hard sometimes to keep silent when things I now believed in were trampled under the foot of ignorance or prejudice.

It was sometime in the late '20s, maybe after the Depression started, when I got a job on a mining dredge over on the Gungarlin River, a bit to the south of old Kiandra. There'd been gold dredges around Kiandra earlier – you can still see the big holes they excavated along the Eucumbene River. The dredge on the Gungarlin was operated by a mining company from Melbourne and a few locals got jobs there. I didn't have much mechanical knowledge, so I wasn't involved with the steam engines, but I'd watch the sluicing screen and make sure it didn't get blocked as the fine materials were washed through it and the gold caught in the boxes below. It was noisy, destructive work – those dredges made a helluva mess of river beds and banks. But money was short and I needed the work. Mum and Dad were getting older and found running the store more and more difficult each year. One of my brothers and a sister helped them but my cash certainly was helpful in keeping the family afloat.

My time at Wonga had led me to think about my own 'native' land, and I wondered about the rivers and the mountains and how they might have been formed. I had some geological and geographical knowledge from school and didn't really believe that the Gungarlin or the Eucumbene had been created by Dreamtime spirits, but nonetheless I couldn't divorce spirit from that landscape either. So when the dredge started chewing up the river I was a bit uneasy, but not so uneasy as to turn my back on the money.

Anyway, one morning there we made a very interesting discovery. It was a misty morning, the sun not quite breaking through the fog that was lying all along the river. It had a real eerie feel to it, and with the chugging of the steam engine and the rattle of the dredge buckets, a passer-by could be excused for thinking there was some sort of prehistoric monster there in the river! Maybe a bunyip of old – on a huge scale!

At a certain point, a large object tumbled out of the screen onto the gold boxes. I called out to the skipper to disengage the mechanism so I could get this thing out. He did that and things were a little quieter as I grabbed my crowbar and levered this lump out onto the dredge deck. I knelt down and had a good look at what the buckets had brought up from the ancient depths. It wasn't simply a large rock. It had markings on it, which became very obvious to the eye once you started looking. It was definitely a carved object of some sort, but just what sort was a mystery. The rest of the dredge crew looked at it too and after some conjecture about what it was, we all fell silent and just stared.

It couldn't have been Aboriginal, because the blacks' stone objects had been small, small enough to carry around as they travelled. Just who, or what, had made it – and it very clearly had been made, not just formed by nature – was intriguing. I'd dearly have loved to ask Bruce about it, but he was dead by then. He'd been hit by a motor car down on the coast road when he was trying to cadge a lift into Eden. It was a hit and run. No one was ever convicted. Just whether it was an accident or deliberate – some people's attitudes hadn't changed since the old frontier days – will never be known. Bruce was also one of the ones who used to like a drink, and whether he walked out in front of the car is also, I suppose, a possibility.

That day on the dredge made a powerful impression on me. Most of the other guys in the crew put it out of their minds, wrote it off as a freak of nature. But I was sure that the carved rock had a different and far deeper explanation, one that escaped our minds then and continues to do so. I haven't forgotten that rock.

25

Speaking of unusual things in the bush, the Ngarigo clan told me about many strange creatures. Whitefellas tended to write these things off, but the blacks believed in them implicitly. I mentioned bunyips before. Stories about them had been around ever since before I was a kid. Mostly they were told by people to make kids afraid of the water and to keep away. But some of the settlers swore they'd seen something. Down on the Murray River, bunyip stories were common and it was guessed that maybe they were seals that had come up along the river from the coast. But Aborigines didn't have any excuses, they simply said it was a bunyip, an actual creature different from anything else, that lived in rivers and billabongs and that was that.

Perhaps the most well known weird animal that existed both in settler fireside tales and in the blacks' culture was the yowie. Stockmen from the 1800s had called it the yahoo or hairyman. Ngarigo and Yuin called it Dulagal. It was said to be some sort of ape, and though I'd never seen one myself, some of the Kiandra people had their stories. Strange footprints in the snow, weird calls, and sometimes actual sightings of the animal itself. There was even a spot out in the ranges called by the stockmen Hairyman Hollow after an unsettling experience there. But usually the consensus was that blokes who swore they'd seen something had too many rums under the belt.

The Wonga people had no hesitation in telling me about the yowie. To them, it was very real and to be feared. They even pointed out tracks when I lived with them down at the lake, though I did find my credibility being stretched on those occasions. Some of their stories I could understand, like some of their spiritual beliefs that emanated from the long ago. But as for a creature living in the here and now, something I'd never seen nor seen any bones of nor any other sign, that was something else. When they told me about their ancestors battling these hairy men, I didn't want to hurt my hosts so I just used to nod at those sorts of stories.

But all that changed one year in the 1930s. I'd been doing some prospecting of my own away out the back of Kiandra, in the steep drop off into the upper Tumut River valley. Of course, that was well before the Snowy scheme came along and there were no roads then, only rough bridle tracks if you were lucky. I had been on my own for a few days.

This evening, it was very quiet just as the last light was leaving the valley. Then my dog, Henry, suddenly looked up, sniffing the air and making low growls. I said, 'It's just a kangaroo,' but he ran off into the scrub. Moments later, he came back howling and with his tail between his legs. I'd never seen Henry afraid before; he was part greyhound and part mastiff so he usually wasn't afraid of anything. But he was terrified. I was a bit worried then and I picked up the rifle that I had by my stool. Over among the snowgums there was movement. Something was there, certainly bigger than a kangaroo. I called out, 'Who's there?' but all that came back was a very strange whistling call, interspersed with several breathy tones almost like a chant. A funny smell was in the air too, musty, almost rotten. Henry was cringing beneath my legs by now. I couldn't get him away from me. I looked down to push him away and when I looked up again the creature was gone. The trees were still. Nothing.

That was a very strange experience and showed me that, like with the stories I was told down the coast, and the experience on the dredge, there is much we simply don't know and much that can't be explained easily. Recently, I've been reading Tensing Norgay's book about when he climbed Everest with Ed Hillary in 1953. The book was in a pile being thrown out by the Tumut Library, so I grabbed it. Tensing talks in that book about the yeti. Both he and his father believed in it. He concluded that 'westerners were made unhappy by the things they did not understand'. I think there's a lot of truth in that. Despite all our advances, the world still contains much mystery. I'm glad that it does.

26

By then, I'd been on a very long ski trip. A Sydney doctor, Robert Schweitzer, was a member of one of the ski clubs over at the Hotel Kosciusko and he wanted to see what the back country was like. By now, the hotel had been built for nearly twenty years and was well and truly established. It was closer to Mt Kosciusko and so the snow was a bit more reliable than around Kiandra where some years you might not get much at all and the snowshoe races had to be cancelled. There was a friendly rivalry between the hotel skiers and us Kiandra mob, especially as we were in competition for the tourists' money. But we respected each other's skiing ability. Dr Schweitzer invited me to join an expedition he was planning to ski from Kiandra right over to the hotel. That was over fifty miles in midwinter in some of Australia's roughest country. Naturally, I jumped at the chance. I was very pleased to be invited.

We weren't the first to do a 'crossing'. Another Sydney doctor, Herbert Schlink, had done it shortly before. And he'd taken a Kiandra man, one of the Hughes brothers (Bill, I think it was) who too was a strong skier. So maybe Dr Schweitzer was following Schlink's advice in utilising a bit of Kiandra advice and experience.

The doctor had several skiing friends lined up for the trip. There were a couple of Sydney dentists, a company director and a theatre producer named Hood who a few years later sadly was killed when the *Southern Cloud* aeroplane crashed in the mountains. So with me that made six. We were all reasonably experienced skiers, though Robert had obviously asked me along because of my knowledge of the country. Much of our route I'd ridden over in the summertime, though I'd skied only part of it in winter.

We set off in blustery conditions from Kiandra. If it had been up to me, I would have held off a few days for better weather but the doctor and his dentist mates had to be back in Sydney by a certain time, so there was no leeway. Also, it was right at the end of winter so the doctor felt we couldn't tarry, and I guess I had to agree with that.

We made good progress out toward Mt Tabletop and then skied down onto the Happy Jacks Plain just as the first day was drawing in. We stayed at huts, of course, as there were quite a few of them scattered through the mountains then, and no one in them in wintertime as they were mostly built for summer use by the stockmen. You'd be mad to camp in tents like they do today, though of course there's fewer huts today and more people, so I guess things change like that. I can't recall the name of that first hut but I think it was the old Boobee Hut, snug under Far Bald Mountain. We soon got the billy boiling and a steak sizzling in the pan. Naturally, there was a bottle of rum to pass around. We were soon snug in our sleeping bags. I'd never seen a sleeping bag until then, because at Kiandra we'd always just used blankets, so that was something useful that I learned. Trust the wealthy Sydney-ites to have something like that!

Next morning right on dawn, I was down to the creek with a bucket, back to the hut, fire lit and billy boiling. Tea, toast and porridge then off once more. I'd heard of the doctor a bit through skiing but I didn't know anything of the others. They all seemed to know about me. That incident at Three Mile Dam had become known far and wide among the snow fraternity. Although Eric Nagle's death still haunted me, mostly people saw me as a bit of a hero for having rescued Giulia and got her and Seb to safety off the ice. Anything resembling the word 'hero' I found a bit embarrassing, but at least it paved the way for friendship on that big trip through the high country.

Sometimes, Happy Jacks Plain can be bare of snow but there was a good depth this year and we travelled well. Our next challenge was crossing the Doubtful River on our way to Mt Jagungal. People who don't live in the snow probably wonder how you cross rivers in the winter on skis. Well, if the snow is plentiful enough, there's usually natural snow bridges over streams. The snow builds up and up on the bushes on either side and then meets in an arch and gets more solid until there's a good bridge that can take a person quite easily so long as your weight is spread on skis and you are not on foot. This time we couldn't find a bridge and we searched up and down the riverbank for ages. Finally, Rupert, dentist number 1, spotted a bridge further upstream. It was very narrow and looked a bit wonky but it was either that or strip and wade the river and none of us wanted to do that. Each of us then gingerly went across, me first, then the doctor and the others. Montgomery, dentist number 2 (who we called Monty of course), was last and he just got across when the bridge finally gave way and fell with a crump into the rushing waters below. We'd been lucky!

We climbed Jagungal for the excellent view from the summit. I'd ridden here before but this was the first ski ascent for all of us. The doctor and I had a bit of a disagreement about navigation at this point so I had to insist that the route I indicated was the right one, and thankfully he eventually backed down. Years ago, back around the time I was born, a gold miner named McAllister had apparently skied to the top, probably the first person ever to do it (the blacks never had skis of course, and some might say they were wise in that). He was a real mountain man, hardened to the cold and to privation. If you look at maps today, you can see the saddle named after him near the top of the Doubtful. Jagungal, like most of the high peaks, had a crust of windblown ice on the summit ridge, so it was tricky skiing, but we made our way along and eventually up to the summit cone. The old trig was heavily crusted in rime, with long icicles built up horizontally to windward. It was a strange apparition, especially as a bit of mist was scudding across like the ghosts of McAllister and co. From here, in between bouts of the mist, the group got their first look south to the

Main Range and Kosciusko. I guess it says something about the times but we all gave three cheers at that moment and passed the rum bottle again.

I knew while I was standing there that places like this had been so important to my Ngarigo forbears in times past. Here, like on the Main Range and other high points, the blacks had come for the bogong moth feast each summer, and to meet other groups to trade and sometimes intermarry. Summer was a rich time for the Aborigines, many of whom had travelled long distances to reach the mountains. Normal tribal boundaries were able to be crossed then as the different clans all paid respect to the peaks, ate the bogongs and had ceremony in homage to Dreaming ancestors. My world was far removed from theirs, yet in some ways it was close. My skiing friends were no doubt thinking their own thoughts on that brilliant summit, far different to mine. Whether you could say I silently said a prayer, I don't know, nor to whom, but I found the experience deeply moving.

From the summit it was a steep and fast run down the southern side toward the Valentine River. Hood and Monty had terrible busters on that run. They were lucky not to break a leg; despite the medical expertise close at hand, a broken limb in that country could be deadly. As it turned out, each man rose from the snow none the worse and dusted himself off, while we all had a giggle at their misfortune, as you do.

When Schlink had crossed, he'd organised for a hut to be built as shelter on that part of the route. So that was our next stay, Tin Hut. That made it a very long day and we got to Tin just as the moon was starting to rise in the east. The sky was clear and the moonlight was very beautiful on the snow. There was no wind and all was silence apart from our skis sliding over the snow and our breathing as we travelled across that winter landscape. The hut's fireplace was badly designed and it smoked like billy-o. We found a bit more tin and a couple of nails and put it under the mantel to make the fire draw a bit better. It was not much of an improvement but at least we were no longer struggling for breath in the smoke-filled hut.

Next morning, we were away early once again and we crossed the Kerries, which again were fairly iced up. We sped down towards the pass since named after Schlink and down along the Munyang River to the Snowy River. There was good snow all the way down here through the forest, and the wood-running was exhilarating. The Snowy was our major obstacle before climbing the other side and heading to the hotel. The Snowy was flowing fast. This was the old river, before the Snowy scheme's dams impoverished it to a trickle. The rapids were huge as vast volumes of water, obviously indicating the beginning of the annual melt in that area, flowed around smooth granite boulders. Again, the doctor asked me to find a way. After a good deal of searching, I found a place where, with a bit of courage, you could jump between boulders and hope you didn't slip on their icy surface when you landed. Slowly and carefully, we made our way across. It was hairy but it was fun too.

Once across, we made the long trudge up and across to the hotel. Weary, we arrived at a place that I'd never imagined. The hotel was a beautiful stone building, finely finished inside, with central heating and comfortable rooms. There was silver service in the dining room and chandeliers. So this was how the other half lived! The doctor now showed his appreciation for my assistance on the trip by not only shouting my accommodation expenses but lending me a dinner jacket so I wouldn't look out of place among all the finely dressed guests. Men wore jacket and tie and women wore evening gowns. I'd never seen so many well groomed people. I was beer and they were champagne! I realised that I had come a long way (literally and metaphorically) from Kiandra.

When the hotel burned down in the early '50s, that was a terrible shame. I know there's lots of lodges and hotels now in the mountains, like at Thredbo and Perisher and those sorts of places, but the Hotel Kosciusko was from an earlier time. It had lots of that old charm which you see so little of these days. I understand that the servants' wing escaped the fire and these days is a lodge. At least something of the old place survives, and maybe it's appropriate that it is the staff wing, because the staff certainly ran that place. Most hotels these days seem to employ hardly anyone, but back in the late '20s that hotel really did lay on the service.

There were a couple of things about that trip which stand out in my memory now, things different from the views and the companionship of the other men and seeing new country. I started to see the fine detail of the bush, and I don't think I would have done that if I had not had that time with the Ngarigo and Yuin people down the coast.

On our second day out, we were heading through this lovely grove of snowgums and I started noticing woodchips on the snow under some of the trees. After a bit of this, I stopped and had a closer look. It dawned on me that the chips were from black cockatoos chewing into the trunks to get at grubs inside. I'd never seen that before, though I'd supposed that cockatoos did eat grubs, but I'd never thought about how they got them.

The other thing I observed was on the last day when I saw this most unusual set of animal tracks in the snow. We all stopped and tried to guess what it might have been. Then it occurred to me – the long curved claw marks were those of an echidna. Those spiny anteaters go to sleep under the snow for a few months but start to wake late in the season in time for the coming mating time in spring, and what we saw might have been one of the early risers that year. My companions were fascinated, as was I, by the marks. I knew that my sense of what the land was, was changing.

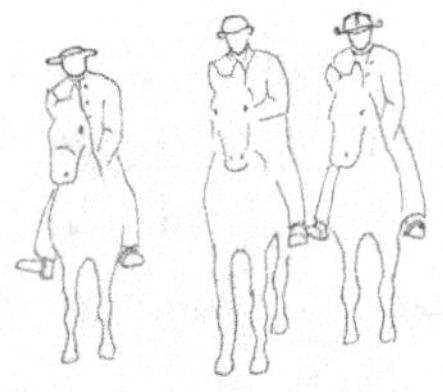

27

That ski story reminds me of a tale from early in Kiandra's history. Many people today will tell you it just doesn't snow like it used to, that it's not as cold as it used to be. Well, I agree with those sentiments, and this story reflects just how cold and snowy it used to be in the mountains. Some time late in the 1800s, maybe a year or two before I was born, there was a group of three American miners working on a claim over on the Six Mile Diggings. The Six Mile is a spot north of Kiandra. Two of them were from Missouri and the third was from Mississippi. They'd been working on the Australian goldfields for years and had been living around Kiandra for about a decade. They had a good claim over at the Six Mile and knew how to sluice and get the yellow metal in their boxes at the end of the day.

One winter evening, they came into Kiandra for a drink. Of course in those times it was never one drink, it was lots of drinks, especially at the cold time of the year. So, when they left to ride home to their huts by the claim, they were a little worse for wear. It was snowy that night and when they got to the Eucumbene and went to cross, it was very difficult to see where they were going. That crossing was a lot deeper then than now, because it's been filled in over the years by all the mining debris. One of the horses slipped and the rider, I think the Mississippi fella, fell in. He was soon swept into a hole by the rushing water and being pretty drunk failed to come out of it. His two mates straight away jumped off their horses and tried to find their friend. They too got rushed off their feet by the river and went into the deep. All three drowned.

When the police eventually found them after four or five days (no one knew they were missing until Dad noticed they hadn't come in for supplies and raised the alarm), their bodies had hardly deteriorated because they'd been in such cold water. The town undertaker boxed them up, and the funeral procession headed up to the cemetery on Permanent Creek. Well, that winter the ground was so hard that no one could get a pick into that cemetery ground. They came back the next day and the day after, but no joy.

So the only alternatives were to leave the coffins there until the weather warmed up and the ground softened, or to take the three unfortunates down to Adaminaby and bury them there. No one wanted coffins sitting above ground – especially the more superstitious members of the Kiandra community – so a sled was obtained and horses harnessed and the coffins were sledded out of town and all the way out to Alpine Creek, where the snowline was that year. Then they were put into a dray and taken to Adaminaby. Adaminaby has a very fine burial ground with tall pines all around; they might even be American pine trees. That is where those Americans ended up, in the shade of those pines. I'm not sure how permanent the grave markers were, so they may not be there today, but the three diggers certainly are. They'd come a long way around the world to end up being planted under trees from their own country. And it was the cold of that winter that was responsible for that.

28

id I tell you that by now, the late 1920s, Giulia was married? Yes, but not married to me. Now, when I look back on that relationship, I'm not surprised. I was always far too timid with her and other women that I've known. I never really made my feelings apparent to her, or to anyone really, so it's no wonder that she found someone else.

Giulia, as I've said, moved to Sydney for her health. She stayed with family and got work there. We corresponded regularly but my letters were usually not very long and covered what I'd been doing but rarely ventured into what I was feeling. Giulia's on the other hand were rich descriptions of her new experiences, and always had something to say about her thoughts and feelings for me. As time went on, she'd ask me more and more about my feelings but I didn't really respond properly to that. I always found it hard to express myself. So I guess she took that as a sign of fading interest, which of course was so far from the truth. We'd had some bad times, like the incident in the stable, and of course that accident on the dam, but there were many good times too when we'd shared things in common and made each other laugh (she had such a beautiful laugh) and I did have big hopes for us. Hopes which I now know were bound for disappointment.

Giulia started seeing a fellow who worked for the Commonwealth Bank. How could I compete with that anyway? He'd be able to provide for her far better than I ever could. So time went on and a few years after she'd left Kiandra she wrote to say that she was engaged. It was a terrible blow at the time, but when I thought about it I was far too slow. Life was passing us both by. Soon I recognised that she'd made a good decision – hard though as that was to accept. She invited me to the wedding, at Rose Bay, but at that time I had no chance of getting away. I'd never been to Sydney at that time, and Cooma or Bega were probably the biggest towns I'd seen, so the Big Smoke was a bit daunting anyway.

I went for a long ride the day of the wedding, but as Mum was unwell I had to be back after a few hours anyway. I was pretty moody that day, and as I had not told the family of the wedding date, they were all a bit nonplussed about my behaviour. That was unfair to Mum of course, and I tried to make it up to her the following day by offering to cook the dinner for all of us, something unheard of. I eventually explained to Mum about the wedding. She put her arm around me and gave me a squeeze, saying something about plenty more women. But as I was now almost beyond marrying age, her attempts at sympathy didn't have much effect.

Kiandra had been getting smaller. Withering as the golden vine slowly shrivelled. Then the Depression came along and suddenly all these unemployed men started arriving. Like on most of the old goldfields, people turned to the diggings to try to make ends meet. They didn't have much money, of course, but government sustenance payments meant they could at least pay Dad at the store for supplies. New mines appeared like mushrooms after rain, you know. Business picked up and Dad was busier than he had been for quite a few years. He was now in his sixties and less able to do all the things that he'd previously done to keep the business going. One thing that was hard was maintaining links with suppliers in Sydney. Previously he'd go up there, particularly to Haymarket, Chinatown and Paddys Market and other inner-city areas to meet with his suppliers. So Dad asked me to go in his place. It looked like I was going to Sydney after all. Sister Belle had already been living there for quite a few years, down in Chippendale with a Chinese-Australian husband; she was one of many Kiandra girls who had left for the city. So I had somewhere to stay, and as I hadn't seen Belle for a few years it would be a nice reunion.

29

It was summer, so getting out from Kiandra was much easier than in wintertime and there were now more cars around. I caught a lift with one of our neighbours, George Doran, who had this truck and was going to Cooma to do some shopping and get some insurance papers signed. From Cooma, I caught the train to Sydney. It was the 1930s, I was in my early forties, it was my first ever train trip, and I was pretty excited.

The train pulled out of Cooma station with a belching steam loco up front. Diesels were still some time off, so this was the time of smoke, steam and noise. As the carriages started rattling and rolling on their way, I knew I was onto another and very different experience. We passed through sleepy Bredbo and passed the Michelago station, with the mighty Tinderry Range just lighting up with the early morning sun. Through Queanbeyan, Goulburn and we were well past halfway. People got on and off at the various stops. Gentlemen in suits and bowler hats, bushies like me in cheaper but respectable clothes, a few stockmen in worn moleskins and flanelette shirts and oilskins, women with excited kids, and a few elderly helped aboard by considerate rail conductors on the station platforms.

Of course, being a new chum to this railway business, I soon did something foolish. I opened the window next to me to get a better look outside. I stuck my head out and straight away got a faceful of ash and soot from the smoke coming out of the loco up front. I pulled my head in real quick, blinking the soot away and coughing a bit, and smelling now of coal. The little boy travelling with his mother on the seat opposite gave a little laugh, which mum immediately scolded him for. But I couldn't blame him. I had a chuckle too.

It was probably most of a day but it seemed like no time when we got past rural Liverpool and soon started heading through Sydney suburbs, like Lidcombe, Strathfield and so forth. Then it was the inner city and Ashfield, Stanmore, Newtown, Macdonaldtown, then Redfern. I was yet to learn that Sydney joke about 'getting off at Redfern', but being inexperienced I nearly did on this occasion as I could hardly contain my excitement about finally being in the famous city. But another passenger assisted me and I waited till Central Station loomed up. I was quickly off the train, and there was Belle and her family waiting for me with big smiles. Belle and I embraced, the kids were now young adults and they looked quizzically at their stranger uncle. I shook hands with Belle's husband Terry. We walked the short distance to Chippendale.

The housing here was all terraces, built probably well before I was born. All two-storey brick with iron roofs, a narrow upper balcony and only space for a pot plant between the front door and the footpath. There was so little space here, everyone seemed to be on top of one another. It was a long way from the wide open views of Kiandra and the high country. Neighbours' voices, dogs and kids could all be heard, and a bit of rubbish lay here and there in the gutters. Still, Belle and Terry had made it home so I couldn't criticise.

Belle and I caught up with each other's news. She wanted to know all about Mum, Dad and our other siblings, what old Kiandra was like these days, and what I had been up to. I wanted to hear how the children were going and how Terry's work with Burns Philp shipping was faring in the Depression. I wanted to know all about Sydney too, but of course there was only so much Belle could tell me over numerous cups of tea before it was time to turn in.

One thing about their home that had caught my eye as soon as I walked inside was the decoration. It was the strangest mix of things, owing of course to Belle's background and Terry's work with a company whose ships regularly plied the waters up to New Guinea, Fiji and other islands. There was an old Chinese-style painting of waterfalls, cliffs and ibis, then a mask from some witchdoctor in the Papuan highlands, photos of coconut palms backing sandy beaches, then behind the bakelite radio a little Taoist shrine of talismans and incense sticks (presumably Terry's, as we kids went to a Christian church in Kiandra). It was an intriguing pot pourri.

In Chinese society, respect for elders is paramount, so I knew that my desire to explore the city and have some adventures would have to wait. It would be subordinated to the long series of tasks that Dad had set for me in connection with the store. Early next morning, I dutifully headed to Haymarket to meet the first of the numerous suppliers that Dad had contracts with.

A rural general store sells just about everything, so Dad's list was a big one. His Kiandra shop sold everything from tea and tobacco to treacle and tin sheet, from matches and milk (powdered) to crockery and crowbars, from blankets to bolts (of cloth and of the building kind), from jelly to gelignite, from flour to footwear, from calico to cowbells, matches to mothballs, pitchforks to pie tins, shoe polish to shotgun cartridges, tinned vegetables, clothing, sugar, hats, shovels, nails, medicines, in fact everything a bush community needs. He even got some of his fresh vegetables – those that would keep – from up Sydney way as not everything could be grown in the Monaro's cold climate.

When I first showed up at the Sydney trading houses, the owners – all Chinese-Australians – looked at me a bit queerly when I said I was a Leong. Of course I didn't look Chinese, so I usually had to explain that I was Tom's adopted son. It felt strange to be saying that, as I'd long forgotten that I was adopted rather than born into Tom and Edie's family. That broke the ice and soon the big smiles came out as Dad was well known and respected among the Sydney Chinese community that he had been dealing with for so many years. That I could speak a little Cantonese and Mandarin also helped bridge the gap.

There were of course non-Chinese businesses that Dad got goods from, and Dad was equally well known by them. Places like Mark Foys and so forth. So when I visited those warehouses, I'd put on the Australian side of my personality. Once again, being a bit of a chameleon had its advantages.

Slowly over several weeks I got the work done, and made a telephone call to Kiandra every now and again to let Dad know how I was progressing. The call had to go through a number of exchanges before it got to home, and there'd be all these women operators along the way, various clicks and sounds. It was like my ear was travelling back across the countryside. Of course, the phone at home was part of a local party line; we were one subscriber among many others in the town. You could easily eavesdrop on your neighbour's call, and they could listen in on you. I often wondered how many of them were doing just that on those nights when Dad and I spoke. One of our neighbours had a pet galah and sometimes during a phone call you'd hear the thing in the background, so you knew that Mr X was having a pry. But the system worked well enough and was a big improvement over the early days before the telephone system came in.

During those conversations, Dad sometimes gave me additional work to do, and so the lists got longer as well as shorter. The Chinese trading community was a bit of a closed shop. You've probably heard of the Mafia in Italy, well, I'm not saying there were criminals, but there were strict rules of how you did business. And there was a bit of a seamy underside to that community, which I unfortunately had a bad experience with, as you'll hear.

After a while, I started to get some free time to look around. I got a chance to visit Terry at the Burns Philp offices down in Bridge Street toward the harbour. As I walked down George Street, I started to glimpse this huge metal arch in the distance. For a few moments, I was nonplussed as to what it was. But I'd heard a lot about the new Harbour Bridge, and at last this was it. It was massive! It seemed to tower over the rest of the nearby city. How a new country like Australia could have built it was remarkable, especially during the Depression. When I eventually got down to the quay, I looked across at the bridge for some time. With the ferries coming and going and all the waterfront activity, it was like I was in another world.

It was certainly another world with all the people rushing to and fro. Sydney reminded me of an ant heap in the bush. Yes, there was that beautiful harbour and at night the city lights were like the stars in a bush sky, but so many people, and all so close to one another. They all seemed to wear pretty much the same sorts of clothes, men with grey jackets and hats, and women in same-length skirts and blouses and with hairstyles all much of a muchness. The fact that the Depression was still hanging on didn't make things any better. Many men stood in queues waiting for work, anything they could get, and women lined up for food at outlets through the city. Sometimes, things got rough at those work queues and when all the jobs had been allocated for that day, fights might break out among those blokes who'd missed out. Needless to say, they still found a few bob for a beer and the pubs were crowded, especially as six p.m. approached and time for a schooner or six was getting short before closing. It was real swill at some of those city pubs.

I'd grown up around people who'd been down on their luck; living on a goldfield, it was hard to avoid people who had not found the yellow metal for a while. In Sydney, the homeless and derelicts were in the hundreds if not thousands. I noticed quite a few Aborigines among them, which surprised me because I didn't know till that trip that blacks lived in the cities. The first time I saw a blackfella, I went up to him to have a chat but he told me to 'Piss orf', as did a few others. I guess with my white features they had no idea that we were in a way kindred spirits. The Wonga mob down the coast with their simple houses were a long way ahead of these people.

Somehow I learned about this organisation called something like the Aborigines Progressive Association. They not only did social welfare work for NSW blacks but were highly political and made statements in the press about how downtrodden the blacks were and how unfairly they were treated, and how it was time they were recognised as the original owners of the land here. I had a chat to some of their people at their office in the city and it was illuminating to see what they were trying to do. The 150th anniversary of the founding of Sydney was coming up in a year or two and they were planning what they called a 'Day of Mourning and Protest' down in Elizabeth Street at the Australian Hall. In their offices, they sold souvenirs made by the Aboriginal community down near Botany Bay, I think La Perouse was the place. You know, boomerangs with little paintings on them, and models of Sydney landmarks made of shells. Those people were organised and I thought highly of what they were doing. I was learning a bit more about the story of the blacks.

I got a nice surprise on one of my walks around the city. It was down the southern end of Pitt Street and I just happened to notice all these posters that had been slapped up on a wall (despite the 'Bill Posters Will Be Prosecuted' sign). I probably would not have looked twice, but two names jumped out at me. It was a poster for a comedy night at one of the local pubs. And who should be performing but 'Dunphy and Gillies, two men with two wicked tongues'. So they had got out of prison and seemed to be making it back in society. I would have gone to see them, but had promised Belle I'd go to the pictures that night with her and the family. I silently wished D and G good luck as I walked on.

30

You probably know that Chinese love gambling. Whenever I was in shops around Chinatown, there were Chinese lottery tickets, pakapoo and that sort of thing. I gradually got to know about some gambling dens too in the back streets. These places were illegal but had been flourishing for years. Whether the police were in the pay of the main Chinese traders I don't know, but I wondered whether there was some sort of official blind eye. There were also brothels, similarly trading with seeming impunity. I never would have even considered using a brothel before coming to Sydney, but now I found my ideas changing. Temptations were everywhere, and I was a long way from home.

Anyway, I found it hard to resist having a gamble and through a few of Dad's work contacts I located one of the gambling shops and was told how to get in. They were expecting me when I arrived. There were two Chinese brothers in charge, Bobby and Jimmy Lee (sons of one of the leading Chinese traders), a couple of other Chinese who I think had been born in China, one called Chen and the other named Wong Gee. There were a couple of other blokes, Australians, probably office workers by the look of their clothes. The group played the old Chinese favourite Fantan, and also Western card games like American poker and blackjack. I'd had a bit of experience with these games at home (not for money of course), so I thought I'd take a risk on a wager.

The Lees provided drinks (imported Chinese baijiu, the real thing) and seemed good-natured hosts. After a few rounds, I was ahead a few pounds and I was getting into the swing of the night. A few more drinks, a few more wins. By eleven p.m., I was well ahead. The other blokes seemed to take it all in their stride, but Bobby Lee's earlier smile was replaced by a tense grimace, which he dropped when he caught me looking at him. Maybe he thought that as a new chum I'd be easy meat at the cards. Just before midnight, I announced farewell and got up to leave. Bobby Lee put out his hand in a friendly shake, winked and said, 'Enjoy the rest of your night, Les.' Maybe he'd been reading my mind, for with my winnings I had been thinking of visiting one of the 'red light parlours' in the neighbourhood.

A particularly fetching young woman had caught my eye earlier in the evening on my way to the club. 'Hello, sir, how are you tonight?' she'd said in a very faint Irish accent, and I'd smiled back to her shyly. Now emboldened by the Lees' whisky and a pocket full of cash, I came back to that address, and went inside. The madam was all smiles and asked how she could help me. The young woman from earlier was sitting on the lounge smiling at me, and I said that I'd like her. Madam obliged and said, 'Deborah, please attend to this gentleman.' I was hardly a gentleman, my Kiandra clothes were only slightly disguised by a new jacket that I'd bought the day before, but it was nice to be treated like something I'd never been.

Deborah led me along the corridor and we went into one of the rooms. Inside, she took me in hand and slipped off most of my clothes. She undressed too but each of us still had something on. Full nudity didn't seem to be the style (maybe in case of a police raid), but we were stripped enough to do what we were to do. She spoke kindly to me and laid me down on the single bed, then got on top. She had beautiful long red hair and fair skin. I was of course a virgin – this was to be my first time. Despite my shyness, I was now very hard. She fitted a rubber on me – something I'd never even heard of. I did have feelings of guilt about where I was and what I was doing, but I'd often heard men in the bush use a common expression about sexual relations: 'a standing penis knows no conscience'. I now knew what they meant. There was no going back.

Deborah rocked on top of me and leant over me, sighing and

urging me on. I felt her beautiful breasts in my hands, the first time I had ever touched a woman's bosoms. Giulia and I had never progressed even that far. It didn't take long for me to reach my climax. After a few moments, Deborah asked if it was my first time, and I replied, slightly embarrassed, that it was. She leant down and gave me a light kiss on the cheek. She really was lovely. Despite the social stigma of prostitution, I didn't judge her. For all I knew, she probably had kids to feed at home, wherever home was in that huge city. And how could I judge her without judging myself?

Whatever thought I may have had that our act was anything other than commercial was quickly dispelled when she asked me for the agreed two pounds, which I happily handed over.

As I walked towards the front door to make my exit, I was amazed to see Bobby Lee at the desk with madam, counting cash. He was obviously the manager. No wonder he'd given me that sly wink as I'd left the gambling table. He looked up at me as I passed and said, 'Having an enjoyable evening, Mr Leong?', to which I replied, 'Yes, thank you, Mr Lee,' and I hurried out. He was determined to get back the money I had won from him, one way or another.

I got home to Belle and Terry's place very late that night, taking care not to wake anyone. The effect of the drinks had worn off and I was soberly considering my situation. It wasn't good to have been identified in the brothel, but given the sort of world that I was now mixing in, it probably didn't matter.

Next night, I was keen to resume a seat at the gambling den to see if I could continue my luck, and take some money home to Mum and Dad at Kiandra. The Lee brothers were not surprised to see me, and the games began. Again, I won a few hands and the night was looking good. Then the card pack was changed, and the pattern on the backs of the cards was quite different to the previous ones. I was suspicious but Chen and Wong and the two office blokes didn't complain so I put up with it.

Soon I was losing as well as winning hands. After two hours, I was losing consistently. Determined (foolishly, of course) to win back my money, I played on. By eleven p.m., I was deep in debt. Bobby Lee said, 'I suppose you can pay us at the end of the night, Les?', to which I said, 'Yes, of course. I have access to funds.' About the only money I had at home in Chippendale was for my homeward train fare and for a present for Belle for having put me up. I wasn't going to gamble that away. I'd have to pay the debt once I got back to Kiandra. Whether the Lees would accept that I found out only too soon.

Bobby Lee seemed to know my situation and just before midnight, as we dealt the last round, he grabbed my left hand while his brother grabbed the other. 'How will you pay us?' snarled Bobby.

'I'll have to send you the money from home, from Kiandra,' I whispered.

Bobby Lee then got out a flick knife and drew it across the back of my hand, hard enough to cut the skin but not, thankfully, damage the ligaments. 'That is not acceptable. But in view of our father's relationship with your father, we will let you go, but you must pay us on our terms. It is a full moon tonight. You have five moons to pay, twenty per cent each month, plus an extra thirty per cent at the end as interest for our, shall I say, forbearance. Or else.' With that, he disdainfully threw his handkerchief at me to wrap around my bleeding hand. 'The Lee way does not usually contain any leeway,' Bobby said, sniggering in a self-satisfied way at his little joke, 'so you are very lucky, Les.'

I quickly calculated what the extra thirty per cent would cost and muttered my agreement. I told you earlier how I got a scar on my right hand, so now you know how I got the one on my left.

A couple of days later, farewelling Belle at Central, I boarded the Cooma train. I was older and wiser. Sydney had indeed been an adventure, not quite what I had sought but exciting and frightening in equal measure. As the train pulled away from the platform and headed off into the night, I had plenty of time to think of how I would repay the Lee brothers. At least Dad did not have to know. Hopefully he would be happy with how I had handled business on the trip. At least in that regard I had upheld the family name.

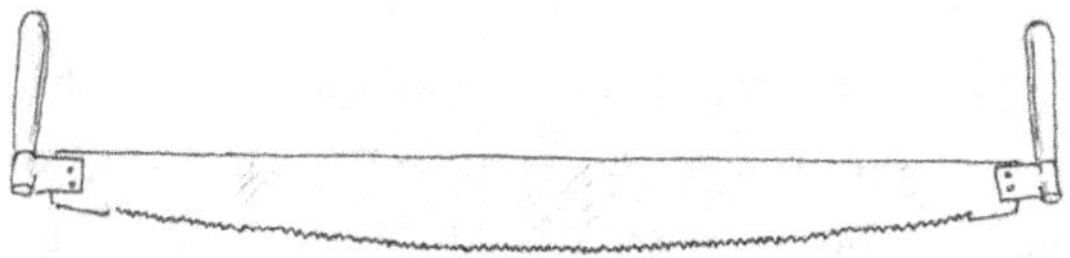

31

At home, Dad and Mum were very pleased to see me. Dad was happy with all the business transactions. He started pressuring me to work in the shop as he and Mum both wanted a bit more time off now. I felt bad arguing against them, but I knew that the shop wage wouldn't pay off my debt to the Lees. It was a very substantial debt, too big and embarrassing for me to actually tell you how big. When I'd come through Adaminaby on the way home, I'd seen old Sam Johnson in the main street. He had run timber mills out in the hills for years. He said to me that he was taking on a few new hands, so if I wanted work he could give me some. That was my best option and that's what I put to my parents.

You may think it a bit strange for a man in his forties to still be so bound up with his parents. But I'd never lost sight of the fact that they saved my life that day back in 1891 when I'd been left at their door. I owed them a lot, and as I was still single it was doubly hard to live a life too removed from theirs. I had absorbed some of those Chinese cultural traits of duty to parents. Anyway, they accepted my proposal to work for Johnson at his mill over the back of Alpine Hill.

My brother Peter was the other single one in the family. He'd always been a bit simple, owing probably to his premature birth. Actually, he was lucky to be alive, a bit like me. Mum and Dad (Mum especially) sometimes found it hard coping with him, so when the mill plan was announced, they asked me to take Peter along too. At first I was alarmed – sawmills are dangerous places and knowing Peter he'd probably start playing with the saw and lose a limb in a flash. But I agreed, to keep the peace as usual.

Peter and I rode over Alpine Hill, saw Sam, and we had a job. It was one of the old-time sawmills, with a boiler, engine and leather belts driving the breaking-down saw and other saws. The milling benches were under this rough sort of shed, with bush poles for the uprights and a corrugated-iron roof. The iron was pretty rusty; no doubt Sam had scrounged it from some other building around the hills.

The saws at the mill were the only thing mechanised. It was still in the days before chainsaws were invented and the fallers in the gang were excellent axemen and could use a cross-cut saw with ease. They would cut what was called a scarf on one side of the tree with their axes. It was like cutting out a wedge, and that would determine which way the tree fell. Then they'd start sawing with the cross-cut from the other side. Soon there'd be this 'tick, tick, tick' noise as the remaining fibres in the tree started to give way. The men then walked quickly back (never ran, in case they fell on their saw or axe) and the tree crashed down.

It was then time for the bullock team to do its work and snig the log back to the mill. I was impressed by the way the teamster loaded these big logs onto the log-drawer and got the beasts to start pulling. Huge loads they were, but the bullocks seemed right at home, two abreast, usually eight or ten altogether, pulling without complaint, sometimes through bush that was hard enough for a man to walk through, though the network of snigging trails made by Sam and the gang had opened the bush up a bit by the time we arrived.

I was working in the mill, pushing the timber through, teamed up with Bert, a bloke in his seventies, I suppose, who'd worked in timber all his life. He was missing two fingers on his right hand, and his left ear. It was pretty obvious how he'd lost the fingers, and those ugly stumps were a constant reminder to me to watch what I was doing and concentrate on the job – otherwise I'd look the same, or worse. But it was the missing ear that had me intrigued. I thought it would have been rude to ask Bert about the ear injury, so I bided my time.

It was in the fourth week or so when I got the explanation that I'd been waiting for. Sometimes during smoko the axemen would have a test of strength, as follows. Each man would hold his axe upright, at arm's length. Then they'd slowly lower the axe toward their face. That really takes some strength; an axe is not light and to do it slowly requires real muscles. The winner was the one who could get the axe closest to his face before giving up. Some of the better ones actually let the axe blade touch their nose. It turned out that Bert had played this game years ago at another mill site but the axe slipped in his hand and took his ear half off on the way past. There was no alternative but to take the ear right off, so that's what Sam did, with his skinning knife. No anaesthetic of course, just a swig of rum for Bert before and after. Due to the high risk of accidents at sawmills, Sam always had a needle and cotton thread to use for stitches should they be required. So Sam stitched up Bert's wound, first sterilising the needle in the fire. Life in the bush in those days could be bloody rough, that's for sure.

Sam knew about Peter's problem and it was good of him to take on someone who wasn't really fit for bush work. Sam gave Pete the job of wood and water joey. It was his duty to keep the cooking fire going, to fetch water from the creek, make the tea and generally help with lightweight menial tasks. That was good for Pete, as it helped his confidence, kept him out of the way of the more dangerous stuff, and put my mind at ease.

We lived in tents a short distance from the mill building, and slept on rough bush stretchers, just sapling frames with calico stretched across and a few blankets and a pillow. Pretty basic but usually you were so tired at day's end that you had no problem sleeping. The best thing about the job was the location. There we were among the black sallees, which are a very nice tree at any time, green grass and a good creek with clean water any time we needed it. The spot was right next to the big stand of alpine ash trees that runs around the southern side of Alpine Hill (and had given the hill its name years ago).

The earliest settlers in the mountains discovered that ash is a good timber for working. It has straight grain, splits easily and straight, and doesn't have any of the warps and knots and crazy grains of many other eucalypts. For me, the best thing about the ash, though, was its smell. Like all eucalypts it smells of eucalyptus oil, but ash is strong, especially after rain. Whenever it rained at night, we'd awake the next morning to this rich smell of eucalyptus. Ah yes, the benediction of the bush, I used to call it. Often too there'd be a lyrebird calling at first light. Those birds are famous for mimicking other birds, but they can copy human sounds too. We heard them doing the cross-cut saw and you'd swear that it was the real thing. It was a magical spot all right.

Things were going well. The wage that Sam paid wasn't huge but it was more than Dad's store would have paid and as food and accommodation was provided, I was able to bank most of my pay. The savings slowly increased and I made calculations trying to see whether I'd match the Lees' debt in the required period. As time went on, I could see that it was going to be nip and tuck, and as I didn't want to take my chances with Bobby Lee and that flick knife, I started punting on the horses to try to build my funds. I knew that was terribly risky, using gambling to pay off gambling debts, but I couldn't see another way. This time, I really did pray that luck would sit on my shoulder.

When I had a chance to put bets on Sydney races through local SP bookies, I'd back horses at Randwick or Rose Hill, and when the races were on at Adaminaby or Tumut on weekends, I'd go down there with some of the other fellers who had a vehicle. We'd even drive to Canberra to the old racetrack at Acton, the one that later went under when they built the lake. We'd all make a few punts. I must admit that even I was amazed by my run of wins. Soon the bookmakers were starting to look the other way when I showed up as they knew they'd be paying me at the end of the day. It looked like I'd be able to pay the debt in time. When I did so, and sent up the final cash payment – plus interest – by registered mail to Bobby Lee, I was terribly relieved. The visit down south by him and his brother that I had lived in fear of for months never eventuated. No more scars on hands – nor anywhere else fortunately!

One thing about those trips to Canberra. The road up from Cooma has a number of level crossings with the railway line. Well, Joe, the guy who drove the car, not only bet on the horses but he would bet on almost anything. He simply couldn't resist a contest of any sort. So if a train was on that line, he'd see if he could race it to the crossing and get across in front of it. As a result, some of those car trips to Canberra were the scariest times of my life. Sometimes, Joe would get over the crossing only yards in front of this loco charging down on us. The train drivers were pretty dark about it obviously, as they'd be blowing their whistle at us and shouting out. One time, I closed my eyes, we were that close to the train – and I was sitting on that side of the car! I could see us all going under those big wheels. Once I paid off Bobby Lee, I declined further invites to drive with Joe to the Canberra races.

There was only one really anxious moment at the mill during those first months. Sam decided to give Peter a bit more responsibility, to see how he would handle it. I was a bit nervous about that but Sam had been good to us and maybe he was right and Pete could do a bit more. Anyway, Sam gave Peter the job of stoking the boiler, keeping the wood fuel up to it and monitoring the pressure gauge. Those old boilers had to be watched carefully, because if you blinked an eye they could blow up. So Pete had this new job and was merrily throwing the logs into the firebox. The rest of us were attending to our own duties. After a while, I thought I should check on how he was going. I walked over to the boiler and the firebox was raging. I looked at the pressure gauge and to my horror it was in the red zone. I flew to the release valve and pressed it. Steam whizzed out in a huge whistle that startled the rest of the gang. I gave Pete a dressing down, much to his pain. Sam put Peter back on billy duties from that point on. Billies generally don't explode! The rest of the gang ribbed Pete about it, calling him 'Gelignite' and things, but it was good-natured sort of stuff, and we laughed off what could have been a real disaster. Lucky, once again.

Many things have disappeared from the bush now. Lots of small animals that we used to see you just don't see any more. Take koalas, for instance. We'd hear them growling away up in the trees in parts of the mountains. Sometimes they were that noisy they'd wake you up at night. But I haven't seen a koala in the mountains for years. Another animal I don't see much now is the native cat, the one the scientist types call quolls; brown-coloured with white spots, a nice-looking little creature. They weren't too popular with bush people because they were always raiding fowl yards and killing chickens. I didn't mind that; fair enough for the bush animal to survive somehow.

But one time near the mill, there was this bullock carcass. One of the bullocks had dropped dead when the team was hauling in a particularly big ash log. Sam had meant to burn it to get rid of it; the smell when the wind blew from that direction was pretty strong, you know. But he didn't get around to it. And one day when I was walking past, the bullock skin was actually moving. I thought, 'Hello, what's going on here?' And then all these native cats ran out. There must have been two or three dozen of them feeding on the carcass. They ran in all directions at the sound of my approach. The darnedest thing I ever saw, I think.

So that just shows you how many animals there were in the bush back then. It has made me wonder about the changes we've made. Even though that timber operation was only taking selected trees, like only a handful per acre, it all changes the bush eventually, I guess. The bush that's out there now is not the same place that I knew when I was a younger man.

One sad piece of news that reached us at the mill one day was in 1937. The mail car called in and had just come from Kiandra. The mailman, Ron Blewitt, told us that the old Alpine Hotel had burned to the ground the previous night. I think all of us in the mill gang had had a drink at that pub sometime or other, especially those of us who'd lived in Kiandra. What was more, all the old records of the Snow Show Club were burnt too. All the records from those marvellous race meets when Charles Kerry and others had visited us and we raced down Township Hill and posed for his photos afterwards. So that was a real slice of our history up in smoke. Little did we know that fire would soon play a much bigger part in our lives.

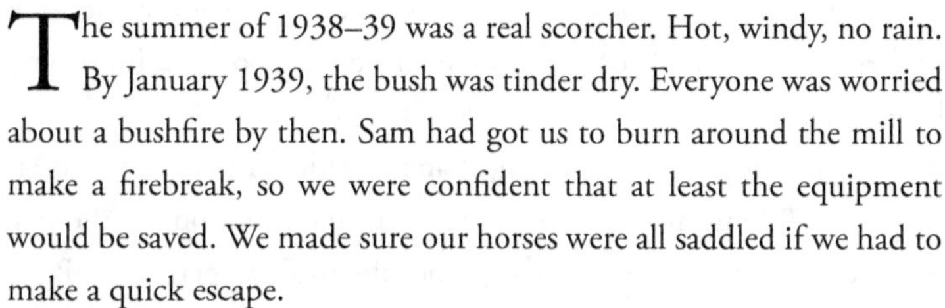

32

The summer of 1938–39 was a real scorcher. Hot, windy, no rain. By January 1939, the bush was tinder dry. Everyone was worried about a bushfire by then. Sam had got us to burn around the mill to make a firebreak, so we were confident that at least the equipment would be saved. We made sure our horses were all saddled if we had to make a quick escape.

Soon enough, fire came. We didn't have it as bad as down in Victoria, where so many people died – especially in the little mountain sawmills they had there – but it was still bad in the mountains around us. First came the smell of smoke, then came the smoke itself. The north-westerly was relentless and we knew that flames would not be long after. Smoke blotted out the sun and although it was midday it seemed much later. Embers started falling around us, miles ahead of the fire front. A big burning branch just missed me, and two of the other blokes had wisps of smoke coming off their clothes from where sparks had landed on them. It was as if some giant was shooting fiery arrows at us. We all doused ourselves in water, and wet everything else we could. The gang had this bucket chain going between the creek and the camp.

Flames appeared above the ranges and straight away we could see the fire was far too big to fight. In those times, all you had was wet bags and green bushes to swat out the burns. We did what we could but it was time to retreat. The horses were alarmed and were stamping and pulling at the reins tethering them to the yard rails, with ears back and eyes wide. They wanted to be off, and when we mounted them it was no easy thing, what with them circling around and us trying to get one foot in the stirrups and swing the other leg over the top. Some of the blokes had a vehicle (the one we'd driven to the races) and they headed off in that. The rest of us made our way out of the forest and headed towards the open country down toward Adaminaby.

When we were out on the grasslands, we stopped and looked up and back. The sky was purple, nearly black. The roar was incredible, much louder than the steam train that I'd ridden in to Sydney. It was a very frightening spectacle. Kangaroos sped out of the forest and were careering past us, and cockatoos were screeching above us. It was hell let loose, it really was.

That evening, the wind changed and the fire started to burn back on itself. Without that, maybe the flames would have gone all the way to the coast, who knows? Naturally, once the road as open again, Peter and I rode as quick as we could to Kiandra to see how Mum and Dad were. Luckily the fire front had spared the town; in fact, it didn't come within miles of Kiandra. So they had a better time of it than we did.

After a few days, when the bush was cool enough to ride through, men went into the mill. The sawmill was still standing, but the ancient stands of ash were now just that – ash. Towering black stems replaced the green forest of before. Those trees were hundreds of years old, and it seemed that it would be hundreds of years again till the forest would regrow to be the same. Certainly, the milling business there was over. Sam would have to move on, as he had done before.

We saw one quite curious thing. In the creek near the mill, there was a small island. Although everything around the creek was burnt, the island had survived. And on it there were at least two dozen black snakes, copperheads and even a tiger snake or two. They had instinctively made for this spot, and here they all were, camped there like refugees. Of course the local kookaburras – those that had somehow survived – had a field day when they worked out what had happened. If you look at a map of this area, you'll see the creek and see

Snake Island on it; when the government map men came through in the 1960s checking their information for a new printing, I gave them that name, so it's now official!

After a big fire like that, the bush is so completely burnt. There's absolutely nothing left on the ground, apart from smouldering wallaby and kangaroo bodies. It seems like the very earth itself has burnt, down to bare rock. It's a hell of a shock to see. It looks like everything is dead and will never be the same again. A ridge line with all the burnt snowgums on it looks like the back of a spiny anteater, all these black trunks sticking straight up in the air. But of course the bush does recover. Within weeks, there were sprigs of green growth on many of the trees, and although the ash didn't reshoot (it has to grow again from seed), the other vegetation was undergoing this miracle of resurrection.

When I saw the burnt land, my thoughts turned to that Aboriginal belief in spirit. Of spirit in the land. And I thought then that that spirit had been destroyed. How could such a blank, blackened, grey, dusty place have spirit? But after the bush started to come back, the plants, the birds and the animals, I made probably one of the most important realisations I have ever made. And that was that spirit was there. It was life. Life does find a way back, and here the Australian bush shows that better than just about anywhere else. I was comforted by that thought.

Immediately after the fire, I felt a terrible sort of loneliness. But as the bush regenerated, I started to feel comfortable with it again. It was sort of like when you have a bad argument with a friend, and then make peace and get on with things. Well, that's how it was with the bush. Spirit was there. It could not be quenched. Spirit was life. Spirit came out of the land and nourished all the different living things: plants, animals, birds, insects and people too, that lived off the land. Spirit connected everything. It seemed to me that maybe this is what the blacks had known, and that some of them still knew. I've held on to that belief ever since. It gives me ease, and since I began believing it I think I've obtained some sort of connection with those earlier Ngarigo from whom my family was descended. I don't say I believe in all the

Dreamtime bit, but that belief in spirit is why, since the fire, I've always remained close to the mountain country.

After the fire, whenever I passed Kiandra's little Church of the Ascension, I looked at the Christ statement on the sign out the front: 'I am the resurrection and the life'. It seemed to me that the resurrection and the life were all around me. It was there in the bush. Many of the locals were preoccupied in the months after the fire with concerns about repairing burnt fencing around their snow leases and doing more burning off to reduce fire fuel in the future. But I was less oriented towards these material concerns. I knew that the fire had revealed to me much more than it had to most of the people among whom I lived.

33

The fire was, of course, a very serious episode and one that none of us would want to relive. But life in the bush also has its funny side, and almost every few months there'd be some instance of humour that would stick in your mind forever.

In recalling the little creek near the mill, I am reminded of the Eucumbene River downstream into which the creek flowed. I've fished in that river on and off for over fifty years now and have had some very enjoyable times. Usually we caught fish, but sometimes we caught other things.

One autumn afternoon, a friend Tim and I were making our way along the bank, casting for trout every few paces. Usually, I fished with bait or spinners but on this occasion I was using a fly rod and flies. I always found that a Royal Coachman fly did the trick with the rainbow trout in that stream, and some of those fish could really fight. They were beauties. With a fly rod, you really have to put some effort into the cast, because the fly is so light. You have to whip the rod back and fling the fly forward to get it out onto the water and to the trout.

Anyway, on this afternoon, Tim and I were casting, each of us pretty well absorbed in his own thoughts and concentrating on the task at hand. Then I had a cast and as I went to swing forward, the line caught suddenly and I knew I'd hooked up on something behind me. I pulled harder and a scream erupted. I looked around and here's Tim with blood streaming from his ear. Evidently he'd gone to pass behind me just as I cast and I'd hooked him in the ear! I walked back to him, apologising profusely, and had a look. The hook had gone right through the lobe. I had a bit of a fiddle but Tim's grimacing showed that that wasn't going to work. So the only way now was to get the fishing knife out and cut the lobe to retrieve the hook. I asked Tim if that was OK and he yelled, 'Just get the bloody thing out!' So I got the knife, gave it a quick sharpen on a whetstone I had in my tackle bag, and sliced as quickly as I could through Tim's ear. The hook was free. Tim grasped his ear and with more expletives wrapped his handkerchief around the wound. I stood back and so help me I couldn't resist a little giggle. The giggle soon became a full belly laugh. I couldn't stop. Tim, bless him, now saw the funny side and we were both in fits.

Tim still sports the scar to this day.

34

With the closure of the mill, Sam Johnson moved out of the mountains and started up again down on the south coast, cutting spotted gum for power poles. That was too far for me to move, so I started looking for another job. Although much of the surface alluvial mining had been worked out by now around Kiandra, there were these seams under the ancient basalt capping and occasional quartz reefs and there were a few mines tapping into this gold, using drilling and stamper batteries and other steam-powered gear. The Hughes brothers and others were at the Elaine mine near the Four Mile, and there was Schaeffers at Larrys Creek, and the Lorna Doone in Duffers Gully.

Another mine, the Daphne, had been going a little while and I rode over to see them. Chester Milfoyle, Bretton Holden and Mick O'Shannassy were running that show. We knew each other – as a son of the Kiandra storekeeper, I knew almost everyone around the district – so it didn't take long to make conversation. I explained that I was looking for work after the fires, and to my relief and pleasure they offered me a job on the spot.

A few days later, who should show up but brother Pete, who sheepishly asked me what was happening. I could tell that Mum had told him to come and find me and see if I could get him a job too. So, I introduced Pete to the others and they were good enough to offer him the billy boiling task, as at the sawmill. They knew of Peter's problem, so obviously didn't want him working at the dangerous end of the mining operation.

The boys had a stamper battery there to crush the quartz that was brought out of the mine, but no air compressor, so the drilling was all being done by hand. That's where they employed me, to work with them on the relentless 'hammer and tap' with steel drill and sledgehammer. One man would hold the drill against the rock, his mate would swing the sledge. Then you'd turn the drill, and hit it again. And so on, and so on. For hours, and days, and days. Then when you had a deep enough hole, Bretton (we all called him Brett) would come into the adit and pack in the dynamite or gelignite – they had both – and do the blasting. The dynamite used the old-time fuse which was lit by hand. Sometimes it went off, but sometimes the fuse would go out, so Brett would crawl in again and relight her and then run for all he was worth back to our shelter. Gelignite was a bit safer, as you set that off with a detonator, which was more reliable.

That's the way we worked. We lived at first in tents, much like at the sawmill. Tents in those days were simply a sheet of proofed canvas draped over a ridge pole that had been cut from the snowgums and pegged down at the corners. Over time, the canvas roof was replaced with iron, and the canvas sides replaced with sort of log and mud walls which made the place a bit more weatherproof and a bit warmer, especially in the winter.

Ever since the earliest days at Kiandra, miners had worked through the winter despite the snow and freezing winds, and we were no different. You simply couldn't afford to stop work for three months and wait for spring. Of course, when the conditions just got too bad, usually during August, we'd clear out back to home for a few weeks. Chester and Brett were originally from Sydney, so they'd head back there and spend a month in the pubs then come back to Kiandra and pick Pete and me up and we'd get the mining going again. Mick O'Shannassy was more or less local, from Adelong, and had been in mining for years.

Life was basic but there were simple comforts. Chester was one of the best camp cooks I've ever met. What he couldn't cook in a camp oven simply wasn't worth knowing about. He'd roast a leg of mutton and it was as good as mum's. Spuds, onions, swedes, peas, it was beaut, and gravy too. Sweets was usually plum pudding, out of a tin from Dad's store.

There was always some grog in camp, but only for after hours. The team never drank during the day. Explosives and underground work are dangerous enough as it is without mixing them with alcohol. Not all mining shows were that cautious and they'd paid the price. Over in the upper Tumut back around 1910, the Homeward Bound mine blew up when the powder monkey, a bloke called Simes, had been drinking before setting the charge. Three of them died. Apparently Simes's head was found skewered on a snowgum branch about fifty yards away.

But even with all our caution, an accident could always be just around the corner. Not surprisingly, the major one involved Pete, yet again. Sometimes, despite Brett's best efforts, a charge just wouldn't detonate. That was a very dangerous time until he could get back into the adit and see what had gone wrong.

One day, about six months after Peter and I had started with the Daphne, we prepared for a big blast. We'd advanced the adit quite a long way and this shot was expected to get us into the ore-bearing ground. Brett set everything up and lit the fuse. We all waited back a hundred yards for the big bang. Nothing happened. We waited a bit longer, still nothing.

Peter at that moment wandered up from the camp and overheard what we were saying. Thinking he'd help out, he started walking towards the entrance to the adit. He didn't know anything about explosives and I was instantly alarmed. Brett, knowing that we still had to wait another minute to be certain, yelled at Pete to come back. Just as Pete turned to answer, the blast went off. Shattered rock and dust flew out the mine entrance and Pete hit the ground. As the shrapnel settled, I ran towards him, as did the others. We didn't know what we'd find. As we got to him, Pete pushed himself up off the ground, dusted himself off and said with that big dopey smile of his, 'Wow, that was loud.' I could have killed him and hugged him at the same moment.

Brett said a few harsh words, most of them unprintable, warning Peter never to be so foolish again. I shook my head as I considered what might have happened. Luck was still on our side.

Once our stockpile of quartz was big enough, we'd start up the stamper battery. The noise was incredible at first, 'thump, thump, thump' as the stamper heads rose and fell, and the 'chugger chug' of the steam engine driving the gear. But after a time, I got used to it and if the machinery stopped suddenly, the silence was a bit eerie. Crushings from the mine gave a nice return of about four ounces of gold per ton of rock. So we were on our way, at least for the foreseeable future, until the vein dipped or ran out, which we were realistic enough to know would happen at some point. Sometimes, we'd fantasise about listing the 'Daphne Gold Mining Company Kiandra, No Liability' on the Sydney Stock Exchange. But like the smoke that rose from Chester and Brett's pipes of an evening, they were idle pipe dreams.

Since my time down the coast with Bruce and the Wonga clan, I'd kept up my harmonica playing and the boys at the mine would get me to play at night. Then one day Mick turned up with this second-hand gramophone, one of the old ones that you wound yourself. So now the music in camp improved a lot. We even had records of Dame Nellie Melba and other singers of renown. I knew Dad had these recordings of Chinese music at home, so one time when we were back in Kiandra, I grabbed one and took it out to the camp, carefully stowing the fragile disc on the packhorse. When I played that and the guys heard this screeching and wailing on traditional stringed instruments and high-pitched female singing in a language they had no idea of, the protests were not slow in coming! Mick said he'd heard better tuned possums than what was on that record.

Since the 1939 fire — no, since that ski trip back in the late 1920s; no, the time down the coast; or maybe even that night in the bush when I was just edging my teens — I had slowly become more aware of learning from my surroundings. I took every opportunity now to try to learn what my world was about, to understand and not simply take for granted what was in the bush, like I had sometimes done when I was younger. Certainly that coast time with the Wonga people had sharpened my skills in the bush, and my understanding of it. There'd be times when I'd see some really interesting things. Like at night when a boobook owl would swoop back and forth between trees above our camp fire. It took me a while but I worked out that it was hunting insects and moths that the fire illuminated. Then I became aware how almost every time the first of us emerged from our huts in the morning, a white cockatoo would screech from the big gums along the hill. He was obviously a sentinel, warning the flock of movement. I also worked out the different spiders and when you were more likely to see them, say the orb spiders and the big wolf spiders. There was so much to observe and to learn in the bush. There'd be the soft booming call of a tawny frogmouth coming through the bush at night, and in the daytime I'd find myself looking at the scribbles on the trunks of snowgums and, if I dug into them, I found little larvae that I later read were laid by a moth. Often I'd say to one of the others, 'Did you see that?' or 'Did you notice that?', but usually the answer was 'No' as they fiddled to get their pipe going or looked for the tea caddy in the stores cupboard.

By now, the war had been going for a few years. We'd all escaped being called up because mining was a protected industry. Even if we'd wanted to enlist, we'd probably have had a battle. Some miners had gone off earlier in the war, but as time went on, the decline in the mining industry led the manpower authorities to tighten things up. Down there in the back country of the Snowy Mountains, we were a world away from what was happening on the front lines. We'd heard about Australian successes in north Africa, then the fall of Greece and Crete, then Japan attacking Pearl Harbour, and coming south. During those dark days of 1942, when Singapore fell and Darwin was bombed and Jap submarines even made it into Sydney Harbour, we were all a bit subdued, and whenever someone rode into camp from town, we'd ask them for the latest news. I couldn't believe that the enemy had attacked that harbour I'd enjoyed a few years before. Coral Sea and

Kokoda, yes, we heard about those battles and things started looking a bit brighter. After the landings in Europe in mid-1944 and advances by early 1945, it looked like the end might be in sight.

Ironically, just as the war news was getting better and better, our prospects were getting worse. The returns from the crushings were reduced to a few pennyweights now. We knew that the Daphne, that golden lady who had been so good to us for so long, was on her way out. Finally in about February 1946, we decided to call it quits. The machinery had just about packed it in too by then, so there was just no incentive to continue. Chester and Brett took down our mining claim sign, and I put up another, roughly daubed with paint that read, 'Goodbye Daphne, the sweetest girl we ever knew'.

If you went back there now, I dare say some of the machinery would still be in the bush, well-rusted of course. The old adit would be there unless the roof has caved in. Probably it only shelters foxes and wild pigs now. The mighty bush will have reclaimed the hut sites and the campfire where we brewed the billy and sang our songs, and heard Nellie Melba singing on windless moonlit nights.

35

Dad and Mum were well into their 70s and still pottering along at the shop. Business was very quiet now and the old town was shrinking with every passing year. The church rarely saw a congregation, and the sound of a mining blast or the fall of stampers was rare indeed. True, grazing was continuing and mobs of sheep were still being driven through town on their way to the summer snow leases out in the hills and high plains. Winter saw some activity. A Sydney businessman called Wally Reed had bought the old stone-built police station and courthouse and turned it into, of all things, a ski lodge. He'd done a good job of it too and made the old cells a bit of a spectacle for the tourists. Wally even had a horse-drawn sleigh, complete with jingling bells. Wally had gone prematurely grey and the blokes around town used to give him a bit of a hard time about that. But his rejoinder was always 'Better grey than gone'. The fellows who were a bit thin on top used to shut up after that.

Dad and Mum both had arthritis and it was almost painful to see them limping around the store, still doing their best to serve the occasional customers who called in. I discussed matters with Belle in Sydney by telephone and I wrote to Jim, who had been in Darwin for years, and to Mary, who had married a New Zealand gold miner and moved to the Coromandel Peninsula back in 1908. We agreed that it was time to give Mum and Dad the rest that they deserved, and that I would take over the store and see how things went. We were all realistic enough to know that the store — and the town — probably wouldn't survive many more years.

I knew pretty well how the store ran and that trip to Sydney had given me a bit of experience in dealing with suppliers. It did take a little while to get used to the new job, and doing the arithmetic when adding bills and so forth was a bit of a stretch, but I gradually got there. One of the biggest challenges was with my hands. They were so calloused from all the bush work, especially the sawmill and then the mining game, that I had difficulty picking up fine things like sewing needles that women would sometimes buy, or fish hooks for the men, and turning over pieces of paper like in the receipt book. But after a while, things came together well enough.

Dad had sometimes come home from the store laughing his head off over something one of the locals had told him. The shop was Kiandra's gossip factory, and Dad heard all the stories going around. It wasn't long after I took over that I started to experience what Dad had known. The locals soon started confiding in me just like they had in dad. Maybe it was the small size of the town, plus a bit of loneliness and add to that a fair modicum of boredom, and you have the recipe for gossip.

Old Mrs Skarsgård used to wander in every second day, completely oblivious to the weather. It didn't matter if it was sun or snow or sleet, in she'd come for a natter. I knew she was approaching when I heard her walking stick clatter against the boards on the walkway under the shop's veranda, and by then I could smell the smoke from the imported cigarette that always seemed to be hanging from her lip. She rarely bought much and I think her trips to the shop were her form of entertainment. She was always very polite and would ask after my parents, who were then spending most of their time up home on Poverty Hill. Then she'd say, 'Have you heard about…' and I knew I was in for some interesting tales. Most of her stories concerned minor arguments between other Kiandrans, and how so and so had fallen out with whatshisname. One wonderful story was her description of how an accelerating dispute between Beryl O'Hanlon and Percy Smith resulted in Beryl throwing a bucket of pig feed over Percy just as he was about to head off to church one Sunday morning. He retaliated that night by letting Beryl's pigs out. She took two days to round them all up from down along the river, but not before Percy had snaffled one for his larder.

Then there was Mrs Petersen (who like Annie Skarsgård was descended from Scandinavian miners who'd been part of the first rush here at Pollocks Gully back in 1860). She was obsessed by her own morality play in town, about who was having an affair with who, and whose daughter was likely to be pregnant at any given time. According to Mrs P, most of the kids in Kiandra were illegitimate. Usually when she was halfway through one of her intrigues, she'd suddenly blush when she remembered I had been an illegitimate baby. She'd apologise and I'd brush off the tense moment with a smile and a wave of the hand. Her stories didn't embarrass me; I was happy to be entertained by her wildly imaginative ramblings.

I was also the source of all fishing and shooting information for the town's youth. Boys would come in with their rods or a pea rifle (the common name in those days for a .22) and ask who'd been getting what. They were all earnest little hunters, so I'd treat them accordingly and let them know where the trout were biting and in which hole a big rainbow had been caught. Similarly, I'd chat to them about where they might get some rabbits or, during duck season, a wood duck or two.

Mountain kids virtually grew up with a gun in their hand, and they were mostly sensible, and good shots. Incidents of people getting accidentally shot were very rare, but there was one very sad case back when I was in my twenties. Two of the Palfreyman brothers had come home from school early one afternoon. Their father had been cleaning his shotgun that day and had left it on the kitchen table to answer a call of nature. He hadn't been expecting the boys home so soon. When Billy Palfreyman saw the weapon, he picked it up and jokingly pointed it at his brother. Whether he meant to pull the trigger or did it by accident I don't recall now, but it went off and poor brother Andy was hit in the chest. He died almost immediately. That incident cast a pall over the town for some time. The family left Kiandra not long after, and headed off to Albury to try to start anew.

Generally, the townspeople were an honest bunch and I didn't have to worry too much about shoplifting. But there was one family who were a bit notorious. I don't like to say it but they were a bit inbred – you know, with buck teeth and those wide-set eyes and a bit of a dim look about them. Their son, Rupert, had always been a difficult kid and he was a young man by now. He might have looked a bit dumb but he was wily. Whenever he came in the store, I knew I had to watch him like a hawk. Often, I'd notice he was looking at me out of the corner of his eye and when I turned away his hand would dart out and try to pocket something. Usually, I saw it and reprimanded him. But if I had to go out the back unavoidably, I knew that when I came back in Rupe would be gone and so would a packet of tobacco or a handful of lollies. There wasn't much point reporting it to the police because the police station had been closed for several years and the nearest station now was at Adaminaby.

Occasional tourists made up part of the passing trade and I'd usually have a natter with them. Like the town kids, many of them were interested in where the trout were biting, or in winter where they could have a ski. Nearly all of them asked about the condition of the roads further on. Some of them had arrived in Kiandra about eighty years too late; they were intent on panning for gold and were certain they could make their fortune. I tried to disabuse them gently, but some just wouldn't accept that most of the gold was long gone. That slight madness that I used to see in the eyes of some of the old timers was evident even in city slickers who'd got a little obsessed about our region's golden past.

When business was slow – which if I was honest I'd say was most of the time – I'd sit on the bench out the front of the store and read the paper, or just look at the view. It was during those times that I found my mind wandering back to Bruce and the Wonga clan and their Dreamtime stories. I'd look down to the Eucumbene River snaking its way southward through the winding valley. Perhaps if I looked hard enough, maybe I could see that the river might have been made by some ancient being after all. I could certainly understand where the blacks got their stories from, and how they explained the landscape. I would look out at the hills and start to see the shapes of some sort of being, maybe a type of super human lying down, encased by the soil, the rocks and the trees and grass. These thoughts battled with the more rational scientific explanations that I'd learnt in school days, but they weren't all that different to what had been preached from the church pulpit when I was a kid, about God and creation in the book of Genesis. There was a quote from the Psalms inside the porch of the Kiandra church, that one about 'I lift up mine eyes to the hills from where my help comes'. It seemed to me that it wasn't a big stretch of the mind to go from that to what the Ngarigo believed. Whichever way I looked at it, I knew that those hills had always been precious to me, that they had been my help, and that my spirit sustained itself upon them and theirs.

Thinking about these things reminds me of a particularly strange day while I was running the shop. It was the second winter and the last one before the store closed for good. That winter was very cold and there had been repeated snowfalls. No vehicles were getting through, whether or not they had wheel chains. The depths were over three feet around most of the town, and up in the surrounding hills there was a lot more.

Anyhow, on one especially cold day, there was this wind blowing from the west. We all knew that more snow was on the way. Hardly anyone came into the store that morning owing to the weather. So I was in there on my own. The wind was building and by noon it was really howling outside. Smoke from town chimneys was flung eastwards with real force. Then this noise started. At first I thought it was just the wind whipping around the buildings. But it was subtly different. The more I listened, the more I could hear some sort of moan, some sort of primaeval animal noise. As it intensified, the moan developed into something different yet again, and now was human. It really sent a shiver down my spine and I still remember how the hairs stood up on the back of my neck. By now, the sky was very dark, the sun seemingly asphyxiated by the clouds. That moan lasted a good ten minutes before it eventually started to subside. When it stopped, all was completely calm outside.

I walked out through the door to have a look down the street. I couldn't see anyone; they were obviously keeping indoors. Later that afternoon when people came into the store, I was tempted to ask if they'd heard the weird noise. But judging by their matter-of-fact requests for goods, I figured they had heard nothing. Not for the first time I was sensing things that others missed. It was another mystery of the bush to add to the tally of all those things for which I had no easy explanation.

On each of those occasions – the unusual object in the dredge, the strange animal that I heard but didn't see, and this very odd noise during the blizzard – I had that experience of the hairs standing up on the back of my neck. That made me wonder why we reacted in this way. I found myself considering whether that reaction was some sort of ancient sense that humans had of the mysterious and the mystical, but which over the millennia we had almost lost.

Well, that was the last winter in the store. By early summer, the writing was well and truly on the wall and I could see no point in continuing with the business. The town just couldn't support it any more. After discussing things with Mum and Dad, I put a padlock on the door on 24 December 1947 (I stayed open till Christmas Eve so the locals could get their fruit mince, tinsel and things). A chapter in Kiandra's history was at an end. The old town was running down, little by little, year by year. It seemed like soon it would be gone entirely, and that only ghosts would wander where once had been the living, and that our lives would be found only in memory.

36

Summer grazing on the snow leases still offered some hope for the district. In the early days, there had been big runs, like Cooleman, Currango, Tantangara, Gooandra and others. But the government was changing things. There'd been concern about erosion from all the cattle and sheep hooves and the burning that the graziers did each autumn to bring on grass for the next year. I recall seeing the NSW Premier William McKell and his soil conservation man, a fellow called Clayton, come through the mountains earlier in the '40s, in their big black government car. They banned the really high grazing around Mt Kosciusko shortly after and declared a big park – Kosciusko State Park it was called then. Many of the big grazing runs lower down the mountains were broken up and the snow leases were redistributed among smaller graziers. Local blokes now got a look in where previously they'd been sort of locked out. So a few new huts were built around the place on these smaller leases and there was an opportunity for me to get some work as a stockman.

One of the people who took up a lease near Kiandra was Bill Jenkins, whose home property was out Cathcart way, past Cooma. The lease was over on Kellys Plain on the upper Murrumbidgee, but you won't find that on a map now because it's all under water since the Snowy built Tantangara Dam there. Bill, like all the other snow lease holders, used the country to give his Cathcart place a rest and to take advantage of the high plains with their acres of summer grass that ran for miles. It really was a graziers' paradise up here, so no wonder people like Bill were excited about getting a lease. I'd known him for years and one day before I closed the shop he called in and said he needed a few hands in the summer and if I was ever interested to let him know. After closing the store, I rang him and we had an agreement.

When I rode out to Kellys Plain, Bill and his mates were just starting their hut. Bill was pleased to see me and I'd brought a few hand tools. We got the frame up and it wasn't too many days before the corrugated iron was on the walls and roof. That just left the floor, which we made from boards split from a couple of trees we felled, and then I smoothed them down with an adze which had originally belonged to grandfather. It had a well worn handle, smooth from years of use. Adzes are very dangerous to use; if you aren't careful and you swing it wrongly, or you miss the timber, you can almost cut your leg off at the shin. It was a standing joke in the mountains that the best way to use an adze was to stand in a couple of kero tins and that way you had some protection for your legs!

Bill had a thousand or so sheep on the lease, so we were busy fencing, rabbiting and generally getting the place set up properly. For me, after a couple of years cooped up at the shop, it was good to be back in the outdoors once again. It occurred to me that maybe that strange sound I'd heard was somehow the bush calling me. I know that sounds fanciful and I didn't really entertain the thought for long, but it does make you think.

Kellys Plain ran northwards into the Currangorambla Plain and it was grass almost as far as the eye could see, with high hills running around the edges. The sense of space out there was tremendous. Of course, the wind used to blow pretty strong sometimes but then you'd get these calm days, and the peace and quiet was just stunning. You could spend a whole day just riding around checking the stock and the fences, and you'd learn a lot in a day like that. I always marvelled at the kestrels that flew above the plain and had this wonderful ability to hover in the air before diving down to grab a lizard or an insect. One day I noticed this kestrel repeatedly taking its prey over to a distant stump. So I rode over and had a look. There on the top of the stump, jammed into the grain of the timber, were all these little skinks. The kestrel was making a stockpile for later consumption. I'd never known they did that until that day.

Foxes were numerous by then and they would attack lambs if they got a chance. So we weren't very keen on foxes, and I've often seen them with a native bird in their mouth, or a quoll. So anything that got rid of foxes was a good friend. One day, I saw a wedge-tailed eagle swoop down into long grass. It was there quite a few minutes, struggling with something on the ground. When it flew up, would you believe it had an adult fox in its talons. The eagle was so strong that it had no trouble flying off with the fox. The last I saw, it was heading toward its huge nest near the top of a mountain gum on the hill slopes to the east. That fox would have fed the eagle's chicks for some days, I would say.

I'd always found eagles a source of inspiration, soaring on the air currents way up high. But I knew others saw them differently. Many stockmen felt the eagles were as bad as foxes for attacking lambs, and if they could shoot one then they would, and often as not they'd wire its carcass to a fence as if to show off. Bill himself was down on eagles and to my intense disappointment (though not surprise), he later shot the eagle that I'd previously seen take the fox. When I found out, I tried to tell him that maybe eagles were our friends, but he laughed out loud at that and wouldn't listen. Once again, I found that my way of looking at the bush was a bit different to that of many of the blokes around me.

Despite these sorts of differences, an enjoyable thing about working on those snow leases was all the people you'd meet. There was such a broad range of bush types. It was a real passing parade of characters, all of whom could easily have walked out of a novel. If you've read Lawson, you'll know what I mean. Evidently, the bush hadn't changed much since he'd put pen to paper back around the time I was born.

One fellow I had heard many tales about was Blind Les Franklin from over Brindabella way. Apparently he could find his way around the bush as good as anyone, yet was almost completely blind. Well, one day he rode in to our camp at Kellys Plain. He was accompanied by another fellow, Jack Maxwell, who used to work at Brindabella but for some years had been a ranger in the water catchment just over Mt Bimberi in the Federal Capital Territory. The two of them rode in casually and we boiled the billy and had a good yarn. You'd almost not know that Les had any sort of dicky vision; he was able to get off his horse just like anyone else and walk over to the fire and sit down. I was fascinated by how he found his way around, and in talking to me he revealed that he used his ears like we did our eyes and that made all the difference. It was also clear that his faithful old horse was another pair of eyes. Les did the mail delivery around the Brindabella valley and it was the horse that knew its way around the various properties. It's a remarkable thing the relationship that humans can have with animals.

But animals can be crafty too. Les also milked the cow at his home, and had a bell around its neck so he could find it. But though cows look pretty docile, this one was smart and worked out that if it stood still, Les couldn't find it! So some mornings Les and his wife went without milk in their tea.

Another chap that I got to know quite well out there was 'Pompey' Elliott, who worked for Bill on and off. Of course, Pompey wasn't his real name, which was Harold, but as he had the same name as the famous Australian general from the Great War he had been given the general's nickname as well. Harold fought in the war too and survived Gallipoli only to be blown up by a shell on the Western Front. He lost most of his right leg and his left hand. Like Blind Les, Harold was able to get around the bush pretty well. He'd swing himself up into the saddle and hold the reins single-handed. When you're riding, you give a lot of your commands to the horse with your legs – you know, pressure from your thighs. Well, Harold could only use one leg so he used the reins a bit more than most of us but his horse was trained well. He had this big bay gelding that he was very devoted to. He treated that horse a lot more kindly than many other bush blokes did theirs. It was lucky he'd lost the opposite hand to the leg because that meant with his good arm he could still use a crutch to walk around. Fencing, drenching the sheep, he was just about as good as an able-bodied man. I deeply admired that.

His injuries brought Giulia to mind. I recalled what she had told me about the terrible conditions in France and Belgium, and all the horrifically injured men that she'd tended.

One day I asked Harold whether he'd ever met Nurse Carluccio.

He replied, 'Les, you've got to be kidding. Do you know how many men were on that Western Front? Thousands. Thousands and thousands and thousands. It was trenches and men and barbed wire for as far as the eye could see. Do you know how many Australians died in the war?'

I said I didn't know but that I figured it was a lot.

'Over sixty thousand,' replied Harold. With that, he staggered up on his one leg, got on his horse and rode off.

I could tell that the war was a subject out of bounds. We never discussed it again after that.

Only afterwards did I realise that whenever Harold handled barbed wire he used to get the sweats. No doubt it brought to the surface uncomfortable reminders of the front.

I mentioned the sense of space. One thing which heightened that sense was the sounds you'd hear out on the plain. On a calm day, you'd hear these beautiful bird calls drifting out from the timber and across the grassland. Tree creepers with their ringing strong notes, magpie songs, the rufous whistler's amazing cascade of notes at the end of their call, grey shrike thrushes and their music, all of them just emphasised space. Then during a thunderstorm, the thunder used to echo from hill to hill. Bang, rumble, rumble, rumble, right around the plain. That was very powerful, hearing that. A bit risky being out on my horse then of course, a bit more likely to be hit by lightning because you'd be the highest thing around. But risk brings rewards sometimes too.

A couple of very sad things happened during those several years I worked for Bill. Granville Street was a nice young fellow with a young wife and a couple of kids. Like Bill, he came from over Cathcart way.

It was generally known that he had a weakness for other women, and played up from time to time, though whether his wife ever knew I know not. Anyway he admitted to me one day when we were chatting while riding around the sheep that he'd got a young Cooma girl pregnant. He was very despondent about it and I think he realised at last that you just can't do that sort of thing. His wayward ways were catching up to him. A couple of days after that, he said to Bill, Harold and me that he had seen a few rabbits in the west paddock of the lease and he thought he'd go out for a shot. We wished him well and said he should bring one back for the pot.

Well, after a few hours, I started getting a bit concerned about where young Granville had gone. So Bill and I saddled up and rode out to the paddock. Approaching the paddock fence, from a few hundred yards away we could see this sort of lump in the fence. As we got closer, we could see that it was a figure. We rode up and there was Granville, tangled up in the fence wires and with blood trickling down from his chest. It looked like he'd tripped getting through the fence. Bushies always made sure a rifle was unloaded when getting through fences because that sort of accident had happened far too often. We were all a bit surprised that Granville hadn't shown more caution. But when I reflected on what he had told me was troubling him I wondered whether what looked like an accident was rather more deliberate. Of course, the inquest ruled that it was an accidental death. We passed around the hat for Granville's widow, as did a number of men from the neighbouring leases.

The other sad event was the death of Tom Raven. Tom was a quiet young man aged in his teens, I suppose. He lived down past Berridale and his father Stan had a snow lease neighbouring ours. Stan was a harsh taskmaster and was always yelling at young Tom. Whatever Tom did it was never good enough. I suppose it was much the same down home as well, and so Tom had been enduring this abuse for years. Occasionally, Stan used more than words and would let fly with a punch. Tom of course just took it, never standing up for himself against the old man. One day when we were riding past them, they were trapping rabbits. Something happened and bloody Stan swung a trap at Tom, just missing him. Bill yelled at Stan to pull his head in and with that Stan used some pretty rough language to tell Bill where he could well and truly go. We rode on.

A few weeks later, we were riding towards their sheep yards. It was the sort with tall posts at the entrance to the yards, much taller than a man on a horse, and there's an overhead wire tie, tied between the tops of the posts, to keep them straight. From a long way away we saw immediately that something queer had happened. As we got closer, we could see that there was a man hanging from the wire. We galloped up to try to give aid. It was young Tom. He was hanging from his stock whip, which was wrapped around his neck. It seemed pretty obvious both to us and to the Cooma police who investigated the death that Tom had ridden into the entrance of the yard between the posts, wrapped the whip end around his neck, thrown the handle end up over the wire so that it spun around a few times and held, and spurred his horse. It was a terrible end to a young life. We never ever spoke to Stan again after that.

Sometimes I've reflected on how fortunate it was that my mother left me on the doorstep of Edie and Tom Leong. If she'd been a Berridale lass and had left me by Stan Raven's door, I don't think I would have been alive very long. Blokes like that shouldn't have children.

We were always on our horses and most of us had grown up on horseback, sort of thing. So when we had some time off, a few of us from the different leases would put on a bit of a gymkhana. We'd make a track and do flag racing and bending races and so on. Some of the better riders would have a go at standing on the saddle at full gallop. That was very hard to do and there were some terrible busters. But everyone seemed to survive and no necks were broken. The other thing we would do is chase some brumbies. Of course Banjo Paterson, who as you'll recall, I met several times in Kiandra during the ski races, made mountain horsemen famous with that poem of his. Many of the riders we knew were just as good as that man he wrote of. There had been wild horses around the high plains for years, ever since the first settlers went up there in the late 1830s. In fact there's a Wild Horse Plain not far from Kiandra, and that was named a long, long time ago. So chasing these horses had been a sport for generations.

There was a stallion and his mob not far up towards Currango and several times we mounted expeditions to try to catch them. We'd get all excited and make rawhide ropes in preparation. We rode out and got onto the trail of these horses and gave them a good chase. But the old stallion and his mares were way too crafty for the likes of us. They'd swing one way and then the other and we'd be flat out trying to keep up. There were some nice foals, though, and the incentive was strong. But we never seemed to do any good. Finally, on one run I was galloping through the black sallees along the creek chasing this lovely chestnut foal. I thought I had her easy but she turned suddenly and I ran into a low branch. It swept me off the horse and I hit the ground with a thump. The others rode up and asked if I was OK. I said yes. They replied, 'That's good, otherwise we'll be a hand short for the drenching tomorrow.' Such was mountain sympathy! But it was just the bush humour. Actually, it took me a while to recover from that fall. To tell you the truth, I was spitting blood for nearly three months.

For the several years that I was on the lease with Bill and the others, the autumn was a busy time of year as we prepared to move the sheep off the lease and drive them back to Cathcart. The high country had always been a difficult part of the world in winter and not a place for stock, although some of the bigger runs had kept cattle year round in earlier days. But the snow lease regulations meant you had to move your stock off the lease by a certain date in May. Usually, that was accomplished without too much drama. But almost everyone up on those high plains had brushes with early snowfalls. We certainly did. The second year we were there, this cold westerly started blowing a week before we were ready to move. The snow started falling a few days later and, boy, did it come down. By the time we were moving the sheep, the snow was nearly a foot deep. It got deeper. The sheep were soon floundering. So the only thing to do was bring Bill's few head of cattle to the front and get them to wear a track in the snow that the sheep could follow. But the worst thing was the rime that would form in the trees. It would build up and then the wind would blow it off. If it hit you in the face, it would draw blood – the edges of the ice pieces were that sharp. That was a heck of a ride. But we got out of it and only lost a few head.

During those years, the stock work left the winter free, so I'd go back to Kiandra then and get some work with Wally Reed at his Kiandra Chalet. Harvey Palfrey took it on after Wally in about 1953 and I worked for him too. I would take guests out skiing, showing them a few basic turns and how to stop, that sort of thing. Wally had me build this hut out on Mt Tantangara so we could take guests on a ski tour and have some shelter in case the weather turned. I'll never forget one time when I was leading a group out to the hut and I had a fall on the way down this slope. I rarely fell on skis and of course it was a bit embarrassing in front of the paying customers. But when I got up, I saw the top of a star picket sticking up out of the snow. It was some grazier's fenceline. Lucky I had missed that, otherwise it could have been a sticky situation with a steel post through my backside!

When I wasn't needed at the chalet, I'd head off on my own on the skis for a few days. Just staying at one of the old huts and reading a bit. I used to read novels, spy stories and crime and that sort of thing, a bit of excitement in the back country. There were always a few copies of the *Australian Ski Year Book* lying around and I always enjoyed reading about the latest goings on in the mountains both in the Snowies and Victoria. Little did I know that soon I would meet a married couple who had featured in some of those annual publications.

By now, Mum and Dad were getting increasingly frail and I knew that they'd have to move away from Kiandra to somewhere a bit gentler. We discussed Tumut but they were not so keen on moving away from the town they'd known all their lives. This was despite the fact that the old store was beginning to fall down, the house on Poverty Hill was missing a weatherboard or three, and old bones feel the cold more with each passing year.

Peter, meanwhile, had moved to Sydney and now lived with Belle and Terry. Their kids had left home and Peter fitted in pretty well, though I wondered how Belle – never patient at the best of times – was coping with her sometimes exasperating brother. Mary wrote the occasional letter from New Zealand, sometimes enclosing photos of the mountains in the South Island, and news clippings. I was intrigued by those majestic peaks and the mountaineers who climbed them. Jim and I had little contact these days. He'd moved to the north years ago to go croc shooting in Arnhem Land and built quite a reputation as one of the best shots in the top end. But those animals seemed to me to deserve a better fate. I got the strong impression that the shooting was really just about sport. It wasn't to eat the animal, or to make other use of it. I found that hard to justify. Also, Jim's few letters to me were pretty racist, which was disappointing given that he had some Aboriginal blood in his family line. He made no secret of the fact that he'd take young women from the Yolngu camp near where he lived and have his way with them whenever he liked – particularly after he'd got on the rum or the gin, which was much of the time. He seemed to have become a real troppo whitefella, in all the worst ways.

37

During my time on the snow lease, one of the problems that Bill was constantly dealing with was dingoes. They would come in at night and kill lambs and even wethers and ewes. They were nothing new in the high country. Since the earliest times, settlers had waged an unrelenting war against these animals. Years ago, when wild horses were even more numerous than they were in my time, it was not uncommon for stockmen to shoot one (there wasn't much sentimentality in the hills in those days) and lace it with strychnine as a bait. In fact, that was still happening in the mountains around Kiandra when I was young.

Consequently, the local dingo trapper was the stockman's friend and was an indispensable part of the high country way of life. I hadn't really given much thought to dingoes until my time on the snow lease, but that changed when I met Fred Falls, the local trapper in those parts. Fred and I became firm friends.

Fred used all sorts of tricks to entice the dingoes to his traps. He would take extreme care in how he laid his traps, and when he'd finished you would never know there was a trap there. He had a special brew, consisting mainly of the urine of dingo bitches (called sluts by the bushmen), which he sprinkled near the trap and which drew in the males. Fred was certainly successful. As was common among mountain trappers, he tied his kills to a snowgum out towards Mt Nungar, just by the side of the bridle track. You'd see this tree festooned with dead dogs, sort of like a horrible Christmas tree.

The thing that drew me to Fred was that he had lived in the bush all his life and had learned so much about it. His observations on birds and animals were acute, and he had things to tell me that I might never have realized. Like the way that choughs used to steal birds from other chough flocks to help them raise their young, and how kangaroos could hold off birthing while a drought was on. Fred knew which lizards gave birth to live young and which laid eggs, which was all new to me. If he heard a lyrebird, he could reel off all the bird calls the lyrebird was mimicking, much better than I ever could. Of course, like most dingo men, he could howl like a dingo and you wouldn't know the difference. Fred had no formal education, he just taught himself. But the thing that really struck me was that he was very conflicted about his dingo work. He killed them very well, but he hated doing it. Over the decades, Fred had come to deeply admire these wild dogs. To Fred, dingoes were intelligent, loyal and courageous animals. They helped keep the grazing animals in a healthy state by knocking off the weak ones, and that went for kangaroos as well as sheep. He knew that he had to kill them to earn a living, but he wished he didn't have to.

Fred was honest in opening up about all that with me, as he knew that any sympathy for dingoes would get short shrift from most of the mountain people. It was because I talked to him about my thoughts on spirit and land and those things that remain mysterious and unknowable, that he was willing to share his intimate thoughts with me. At last I had found someone who felt toward the high country like I did. It was like a breath of fresh air getting to know Fred – although 'fresh air' was not normally a term you would use in connection with a dingo trapper, who usually smelt of dog piss and death.

It would be impossible to say how old Fred was at that time. He was deeply suntanned and sun-lined, with sharp wrinkles around his eyes, and a permanent set of whiskers on his chin and cheeks. I don't really know what colour hair he had as I never saw him without his hat, a battered old Akubra that was sweat-stained and torn from years of wear and tear. His horse and packhorse were always in good shape. He depended on them and much of the time they were his only company, so he cared for them as if they were part of his family. Come to think of it, they were his family.

I last saw Fred one day about twenty years ago in the main street in Tumut, Wynyard Street. He had grown too old for the bush and came down here to have a bit of comfort in his declining years. I wasn't to know then that Tumut would be the place that I was destined for too.

38

It wasn't long into that period working with Bill when we had everything going OK on the lease and there was a chance to get away for a couple of weeks one summer. It must have been about 1948. I took the opportunity to head off toward Mt Jagungal to do some prospecting. I hadn't been out with the gold pan for a while so it was good to check some creeks that I'd long thought worth a look at. So I was camped over that way and one day I heard this engine approaching. This seemed mighty strange because up to that time, away from the few roads in the mountains, there were no vehicles. I scanned the landscape from this small hill I was on and lo and behold I saw a pair of jeeps making their way around the sphagnum swamps and through the snowgums. I had to know who it was, so I rode over on my old horse, Molly. I got to the jeeps just as the occupants stopped to make camp for the night.

I introduced myself and was delighted to find that the travellers were Tom Mitchell and his wife Elyne, from Towong Hill station on the upper Murray. With two friends, Ossie Rixon and Bill Littlejohn, they were making an epic drive over the mountains, the first persons probably to ever do such a journey not on a horse or skis. Oh yes, and the other member of the expedition was Elyne's sheepdog Roley. Tom's name was well known to me because he had been quite a famous skier, a champion racer and a tourer and like me had done some long trips in the mountains. By now, he was a Victorian parliamentarian and a pretty quirky sort of character. Later, he developed a reputation for knitting during parliamentary debates!

As I got yarning with them, I recognised Elyne's name now too. She and Tom had written articles in the *Ski Year Book* and she was a very good skier in her own right, having toured with Tom and won an international downhill event, I think, in Canada before the war. What I hadn't heard was that Elyne was now writing books. She told me about her first one, *Australia's Alps*, which I knew I would have to buy because it dealt with her and Tom's many ski trips and summer journeys in the mountains. Her enthusiasm for the mountain life was infectious and she spoke with a smile and a sparkle in her eye.

As the conversation continued, Elyne explained that at the end of the war her second book, called *Speak to the Earth*, had appeared. As she talked, I could see that we were very much kindred spirits. Her love of the land and her seeking after some sort of spiritual value in the mountains spoke to me immediately.

'The mountains are very, very dear to me,' she said. 'We look out at them every day from Towong Hill and whenever I'm in them I get a strong feeling of being in a place with an extremely deep past. The mountains have an elusive meaning for me that I find hard to pin down. I guess that's why I'm so intent on being in them as often as I can, and continuing with my writing about them. I'm always looking for that special place where this meaning might be revealed.'

As she spoke, I could see that her view of the mountains was almost mystical.

Meanwhile, Tom's eyes had started to glaze over and I could see that his more practical views on things were not the same as his wife's. He excused himself to go and check something in the jeeps. I explained to Elyne my own views and how my time with Ngarigo people had led to new insights. She had absorbed many stories of the blacks both from her own family's grazing history up around Tabulam and the Clarence valley, and from Tom's family who had been in the upper Murray for generations.

I put my foot in it at one point when I said that I had worked at one of Sam Johnson's sawmills. Elyne immediately cried 'Vandalism!'

and explicitly expressed her concern about tree clearing and the loss of soil that resulted. She felt that Australians had cut down too many trees and unless we changed our ways we were doomed to the same fate that had claimed many earlier civilisations. She had written a book on that theme too, which I think was called *Soil and Civilization*. Her argument stayed in my mind and I must admit that in time I came to look on my sawmill days in a new light. That's why I commented earlier on the sorts of changes that we probably brought to the bush through our timber-getting.

By now, the moon was well up and the meal that the travellers had kindly shared with me was over. Molly was snuffling impatiently over on the edge of the firelight so it was time to head back to camp. During the chat, Tom and Elyne had asked me about my life in Kiandra and my recollections of skiing in that part of the mountains. They were evidently impressed, because a little later they mailed to me an advance copy of the latest *Ski Year Book* with an article they had written, based on our chance meeting out in the Jagungal wilds. The article was titled 'Les Leong: Kiandra's keeper of the skis'. I was quite touched by that. It was probably the only time my name ever appeared in print.

That meeting with Elyne Mitchell gave me encouragement in my own views about the mountains. She was just as enthusiastic about nature as I was, and as observant too; I remember her talking about her favourite azure kingfishers along the Murray where she lived, and how she could study them for hours. Her private search for meaning, her sense of being held captive by the high country, the way the mountains pulled at her heart all struck a strong chord with me. As with Fred Falls, it was very good to know that there were some of us about who felt these sorts of things.

39

The Mitchells' jeeps were the first motor vehicles to cross the mountains, and it soon became apparent to me that they were at the beginning of a new age in the high country, a new age that I never would have foreseen. Only a year after I met Tom and Elyne and their two friends on their trans-mountain journey, the mighty Snowy Mountains Hydro Electric Scheme got underway. Soon there would be many more roads and vehicles in the high country, the wild high country that I had known since I was a kid.

I've said a few times that the high country is a great place of water. There's always pure fresh water in the creeks and rivers, even during the worst of droughts. It had long been mooted that a scheme should be built to use some of that water, either for irrigation in the west or for electricity. The mountain people, many of whom had never had electricity in their lives, were pretty sceptical of those plans. But in 1949 they had to eat humble pie because the government made a start with the Snowy.

Bill Jenkins gave up on the snow lease about 1954. So I was looking to make a quid again. By then, the Snowy was getting into full swing and the first of their power stations was almost finished over at Guthega – on the route that I'd skied with Dr Schweitzer in the late 1920s. I went down to Cooma and presented myself at the Snowy's employment office. Just as I was filling in the paperwork, the Snowy commissioner, William Hudson (he later became Sir William), saw me at the counter as he was hurrying past. He overheard me telling the employment officer about my bush experience, on horseback and skis. The officer was a bit dubious about my age (which I'd lowered a bit and said was fifty-three not sixty-three – my jet-black hair helped me there) but Mr Hudson butted in and said, 'Sounds like a good man for us. Give him a job.' So I could say that I was appointed directly by Snowy Bill himself! He was a no-nonsense sort of fellow and I was indebted to him.

The Snowy's work in the upper Tumut River region was underway and although much of the surveying and planning had been done, there was still some of this pioneering activity going on and my first job was to take survey parties and some of the water-gauging teams into that area. The Tumut valley is extraordinarily steep in places and horses were the only way in before road construction. So the journeys required some skill on horseback. The men doing the work had a bit of experience but I had to take it easy with them. They were a motley crew, from about five nationalities. Unbeknown to me until I joined the Snowy, great numbers of Europeans had come out to Australia after the war, seeking to rebuild their life, and many of them were on the Snowy. When I heard that this survey group included Germans, a Pole, a Brit plus an Italian and a Yugoslav, I thought all hell would break loose at the drop of a hat. But it was a great credit to the Snowy that people who had been bitter enemies just a few years earlier were now working together in harmony on our side of the world.

When we were in camp together and chatting around the fire (so many of my life's nights had been spent just like that – sitting around a fire in a bush camp), we naturally avoided talking about the war. Given that Rolf, Wolfgang, Bruno, Waldec, Antonio and Brian had all been at each other's throats one way or another during 1939–45 we steered clear of any reference to the conflict. The one subject that was discussed over and over was each man's hope for the future. Rolf and Wolfgang were both single but had already dated local girls during their free time when in Cooma. Both of them were enamoured of Australian females, and I wished them luck. Cooma by then was a changed town to the place I had known, what with nightclubs and big-name bands visiting from Sydney. You could have a dance almost any night of the week. It almost made me think about heading down there with the mouth organ and seeing if I could get on the bill.

Antonio (who we just called Tony, of course) and Waldec both had sweethearts back in their home countries. In Tony's case, his fiancée waited in Naples and Tony had hopes of being able to finance her emigration in a year or two. Waldec had a wife and a child still waiting in a refugee camp but he had already booked their passage; of the group, he had been with the Snowy the longest and had diligently saved his pay, which was not inconsiderable as the Snowy paid good wages. Brian was undecided about whether he would stay in Australia but as time went on he confided to me that the climate was starting to claim him and he thought he could see a long-term future here. That the vagaries of our mountain weather were an attraction to him indicated to me what he had put up with in the home country, which was apparently somewhere bleak up in Yorkshire.

One funny aspect of that early work was that Wolfgang and Rolf were very precise about the way they undertook the surveys. They used to get a bit frustrated with the rest of us (as well as being a horseman and guide for the gang I was also a chain man) and every so often would give us a little lecture in their broken English about the need for precision in the measurements and how we recorded them. I took it with a grain of salt, but the others sometimes got a bit hot under the collar, you know, with the Germans lording it over them. Usually, it passed off in a minute or so, and soon we were all best of mates once more. My use of the word 'mate' soon caught on with the others and it amused me to hear them using it in their varied accents. 'You're becoming Australian, mate,' I'd say, and they would grin proudly.

At night, we'd look up into the sky. The stars were familiar to me but foreign to the boys from Europe. I would point out the Southern Cross and explain its significance to most Australians. They would tell me about their northern stars. Then we'd just sit in silence and enjoy the unbounded vista. It didn't really matter whether one was under recognisable stars or not; the beauty of it all overcame whatever national boundaries humans had created for themselves.

The survey work went on for a time before I was absorbed into the construction workforce building the dams up in that area. Tumut Ponds and Tooma were the main dams constructed to catch the water for the upper Tumut power stations and for irrigation schemes out in the Riverina and beyond. I had never worked with concrete before and it was an interesting experience. My bush skills were a bit out of their depth up there but nevertheless I was able to pull my weight with the other workers. As the dam walls rose, I started to get an idea of the scale of the project and I could see that the mountains would not be the same again. So I felt anxious about that, a bit conflicted like Fred Falls was about killing dingoes. I could feel that wagging finger again, that nagging conscience that I'd first felt by the Eucumbene River during sluicing. But like everyone else I needed a pay packet, and I hoped the high country would survive. It had outlasted gold miners, and grazing by then was being further phased out for expansion of the Kosciusko Park, which seemed to go hand in hand with the scheme as the engineers didn't want any silt in their dams.

So what we humans did to the high country perhaps was small in the longer scale of time. The mountains were changing, that's for sure, but I felt that they would still be there at the end of it all. At least, I hoped they would be. I decided that the expansion of the park was something I had to agree with, for although I'd worked with stock and dug for gold and sawn down trees, I could see that we had to work with the land not against it. I think if Bruce had lived to see the park he would have approved of it. Few mountain people welcomed the park, as they saw it closing off the mountains to them. I could sympathise with that view too, but I felt we had to look beyond that and into the longer term. As often in the past, I didn't voice my thoughts unless I knew just who I was talking to.

It was hard work on the Snowy scheme but it had its compensations. As I've said, the pay was good, and the companionship was strong.

Having grown up in a town with different nationalities, I had little trouble bending my ear to the various languages and accents on the work site. Some of those guys looked to me as an interpreter, which was pretty funny at times. Like trying to get an Italian and a Serb to cool down when each thought the other was cheating at cards. About the only sort of conflict on the scheme that I was aware of was when two particular rival European groups, who I'd better not name, had a go at one another, usually by doing a midnight raid on the avenue of national flags in Sharpe Street, Cooma, and tearing down the other mob's flag.

At knock-off time, we adjourned to the wet canteen. The number of beers that those men sank was phenomenal and the waitresses used to carry these massive trays with a dozen schooners each or more. They were good nights and a way for all those mainly single men to dowse their loneliness in this foreign land that they were so desperate to make their new home. In contrast to them, I was right at home. Many of those Europeans were sort of envious of me for having spent all my life in the mountains, that for me this was all familiar and yet for them was so strange and confronting, at least until they started to get the place under their skin. Most of them had clippings pinned up in their huts of scenes from home, and a letter from family almost resulted in tears. It soon occurred to me that they were very brave, having embarked on this big adventure, one in which they really had no choice, as staying home was a dead end, and Australia represented the light at the end of a terrible war-torn tunnel for them and their families.

In 1958, there was a bit of a stir when one of the carpenters found the remains of a plane that had disappeared back in about 1931. I've mentioned before that Clyde Hood was one of the skiers on that late 1920s ski trip from Kiandra to the Hotel Kosciusko and that he lost his life in the *Southern Cloud*. Well, it was that aircraft that had been discovered. The carpenter was Tom Sonter, who'd I'd met once or twice and quite liked. He loved the bush and used to get out and do some walking and photography whenever he had a day off. He'd gone on a walk this day in the incredibly rugged upper Tooma River country where they were working. Completely by accident, he stumbled onto the wreckage and solved the mystery of an aircraft that had been missing for nearly thirty years. Once the plane was positively identified by aviation officials as the *Southern Cloud*, truckloads of Snowy workers headed up there and trekked into the site to claim a souvenir. Lots of journalists arrived too to cover the story for the big papers. Most of the wreck was taken out in small bits in men's pockets, though the Cooma Lions Club got part of it for their memorial. I didn't go in there because I felt that it didn't really show respect to the dead, especially as I had known one of the passengers. Also, I heard that some men souvenired human remains – pieces of bone and suchlike – which I thought was appallingly ghoulish.

The Snowy had a pretty good safety record, but many workers took terrible risks. Dam building and that sort of thing was known to be tough – there was this saying that came to us with the Americans I think, about 'a man a mile', meaning the death toll could be high indeed. I saw men walk out along beams way above the ground, ride the concrete buckets out over dam walls, and work in tunnels blithely dodging the railcars that brought out the mullock. Many of those fellows were lucky to be alive. There were terrible stories of blokes being entombed in wet concrete and their bodies never found. I can't vouch for the truth of those tales, but I think the official figure was about a hundred and twenty deaths on the scheme. I considered myself fortunate not to have witnessed one of those fatal accidents. I had seen a few dead bodies in my time since that landslip among the Chinese miners all those years ago and I didn't relish seeing any more.

By the early 1960s, work in the upper Tumut was reaching completion. Whenever I told other workers on the scheme that I was now seventy-one years of age, their faces twisted into a look of wonder then of humour as they exploded into laughter and thought I was pulling their leg. When I finally convinced them that I was telling the truth, they simply couldn't believe it. The other thing they couldn't believe was that I had never owned nor driven a car. I think they saw me as a bit of a museum piece. And maybe I was.

40

Meanwhile, Mum and Dad had got too old for the house at Kiandra. It was just too hard for them to deal with the climate, to keep themselves stocked with firewood, and to drive into Adaminaby, and often Cooma, in their old car and with failing eyesight. I could only do so much for them as I had been away in the Snowy work camps for such long periods. Eventually, they agreed to move down to Tumut.

They got this nice little place in Dalhunty Street. I would visit them and see that they were OK for provisions and I would mow the lawn, do any radio or other little repairs for them (Snowy blokes showed me a few tips with electrical goods and a soldering iron). I would try to drop in about every few weeks. We'd usually talk about old Kiandra days, about the snow (which they felt didn't seem as deep any more, and neither did I for that matter), about any news from other people who they had known and who'd left the town, and about my work with the Scheme. Like me, Mum and Dad were in two minds about the Snowy, though for different reasons. They could understand the national benefits, but what benefits it held for the mountain people were difficult to see.

Mum's mind was starting to go. She could remember the early days real well, but she'd forget what she asked me to buy for her the week before. Eventually, she had trouble recognising me when I arrived at the front door, which was heartbreaking. The woman who had rescued me in the '91 blizzard was slipping fast. When she died in 1959, she died in Dad's arms in their double bed. She was a beautiful woman, and one who had given me everything.

Dad went on on his own for a time. Shuffling through the house in his slippers, reading Chinese language newspapers he subscribed to in Sydney, as well as the local Tumut paper, even going fishing with me once in the Tumut River. As the river was soon to be changed forever by the Snowy scheme, we thought we should have a last visit to some of the spots that were destined to be drowned. We had a lovely morning along the river beside Brandy Marys Flat, and Dad caught a couple of rainbows which delighted both of us. If you go to Brandy Marys today, you'd need scuba gear!

Dad's lungs had not been good for some years and he gradually declined further. With Mum gone, a light had gone out. She wasn't there any more and he felt like part of him was already in the grave. Belle and Peter got down from Sydney once and that meant a lot to Dad but it was to be the last time he would see them.

Luckily, I was staying with Dad at the end. He'd been coughing badly through the night and I took in some of his medication around two a.m. He was a bit more comfortable after that. Just on dawn, I heard him call me. When I entered the room, he was just staring up at the ceiling. As soon as I looked into his eyes, I could see that life was gone. The soul had passed away. I checked for breath and pulse, but to no avail. I said a silent prayer and clasped his hands for about half an hour before I rang the police.

I had seen this moment coming for some time of course and had collected several nicely shaped small stones from around Kiandra and a couple of daffodil bulbs from the old garden at Poverty Hill. I also found one of Dad's old hats in the store, which was now a fallen ruin. The hat sat on Dad's coffin during the church service. At the cemetery, as Dad's coffin was placed into the grave, I threw the stones and bulbs down after it. Another part of old Kiandra was gone. At least Dad and Mum are buried together in the old cemetery at Permanent Creek.

The past had always seemed close to me. But with Mum and Dad now dead, the past seemed distant, it seemed remote, and the world around me was continuing to change.

41

My work with the Snowy didn't keep me away from Kiandra all the time. When I had the chance, I would stay in the old home, despite the weatherboards coming off the walls and a bit of flapping iron on the roof. In fact, the first thing I would do on arrival was get out the tool bag and make a few repairs. I kept in contact with Harvey Palfrey and whenever an opportunity presented itself, I gave his guests a bit of ski tuition.

His place was now called the Kiandra Chalet Hotel and since he'd got a liquor licence the lodge had livened up considerably. Snowy workers used to frequent the bar, both in search of drinks and some female company, what with all the skiers there in the winter. The Kosciusko State Park Trust actually owned the building (Harvey, I think, leased it) and they decided to upgrade the place. By the early 1960s, it was double-storey and with lots of guest rooms. I'd heard about the growing ski resorts over towards Mt Kosciusko, like Thredbo, Charlotte Pass, Perisher and Smiggins, and maybe the trust was trying to spread the tourists around the park a bit. Some of Kiandra's better skiers in earlier days, people like brothers Jim and Bill Pattinson, used to go over that way to ski and they won races at Charlotte Pass after the chalet was built in the 1930s, which did Kiandra proud. But I was never interested in competing very much, not on that scale anyway, and didn't get over that way except for that long trip with the doctor and the others in the late '20s. I guess I just liked the Kiandra hills and their hidden valleys.

Anyway, Harvey's place used to really jump on Saturday nights and was quite a nightspot. Perhaps a little of that old Kiandra spirit of the gold rush days had come back. A few Snowy workers, led by an Irish bloke called Ulick O'Boyle, formed a band called The Settlers around that time and Ulick obviously knew Kiandra, and Harvey's hotel, pretty well. In one of his songs, he had a line about 'Harvey's college of carnal knowledge'. Whenever Snowy blokes heard that, they would have a giggle and cast knowing glances. For me, the line brought back that memory of Giulia and the Sydney fella out in the old pub's stable. The stable might have burnt down in 1937 with the rest of the Alpine, but the memory remained with me. I met Ulick a few times. Typically Irish, he was a warm-hearted fellow with a great singing voice too, but stubborn and a bit pugnacious – he'd been a good boxer in his time.

I had to admit that I was getting too old to continue any longer with the Snowy work, but I was still able to take people out on the skis at Kiandra in the winter time and, as I've mentioned, Harvey was happy to have me around. By now, there was a T-bar tow on the old Township Hill ski slope. The days of having to walk your way up the slope on your skis were slipping further behind, at least for the majority of tourists who preferred their skiing on this home slope. For those who were a tad more adventurous, I'd lead them out like a mother duck with her ducklings (a rather old mother duck, I might say!) and we'd have some fun, sometimes even getting as far as the hut on Mt Tantangara. If it was a windy day with a bit of snow blowing, we'd boil up some soup in the hut. Those Sydney visitors really thought that was great, and wanted to know all about Kiandra's history, which I was happy to regale them with. Most of them found it almost unbelievable that people had mined gold and lived in tents in those conditions. In fact, they had a hard time comprehending that a few of us still lived in the old town. They'd comment on the derelict look of most of the remaining houses. I bit my tongue rather than admit which one I actually lived in.

Some of the more observant skiers noticed that I never carried a map and rarely looked at the compass that hung on a cord around my neck. I explained that I'd lived in these hills all my life and didn't need maps. They looked a bit sceptical at that, but followed on nevertheless. If the cloud came down, they'd always ski a bit closer to me.

Despite the decline of the town, there were a couple of new buildings. The Kiandra Pioneer Ski Club was still in existence and now had its own club hut. People like Peter Fountain and Colin Myers were a ball of energy and for a little while Kiandra was looking grand once again. Another club, called Wolgal after the Aborigines, built their lodge next to Pollocks Gully, not far down the hill from Jim Pattinson's place.

A few celebrities even came to town and stayed at Harvey's hotel. One of them was a famous painter named William Dobell. He was a great portraitist, as you may know. Apparently, he had won a big prize up Sydney way, called something like the Archibald. I don't recall what it was that brought him here but he seemed a nice enough fellow. A little later, it was decided to make a movie in Kiandra, or at least to make part of it there. Harvey was a great entrepreneur and I guess it was he who somehow manoeuvred these things, and got the film company to stay in Kiandra for that part of the filming. The movie was about Ned Kelly, who of course anyone from Kiandra had heard of. But they got this little English guy to play the part. I'm told he was a singer with a modern band and I think his name was Mick Jagger, though I'd never heard of him up to that time. Personally, I thought he was a bit scrawny to play a tough Irish-Australian like Kelly. When some of the Sydney skiers heard about this Jagger, they got really excited. They all seemed to know his name. Perhaps that indicated how cut off from the rest of the world I had been. Yes, a museum piece after all! That would have been about the end of the '60s, I would say. I would like to have seen the finished film but never got around to attending a cinema, which would have meant quite a long trip by then.

I've said that the snow didn't appear to be as deep any more. Well, in 1964 the snow gods intervened and it just bucketed down.

It snowed and snowed and snowed, all around the mountains. It was not just feet deep, it was yards deep in places. The mountains had not looked as good in years. I hoped it might be a return to the old days, but the following years were disappointing by contrast. We went back to having periodic years of poor snow on the Kiandra hills, and sometimes it seemed they got poorer the longer time went on.

42

I gave up on the skiing when I turned eighty. I just found the old bones a bit too weary to keep it up, though putting the skis away was a sad moment, I can tell you. I wrote a letter to Elyne Mitchell then and she sent a kind reply, telling me I had led a wonderful life in the mountains, and saying she hoped she would still be skiing at my age. By then, Elyne was quite famous; her Silver Brumby books were being read by children right around the world. Harvey had left Kiandra the previous year to open Providence Lodge on the shore of Lake Eucumbene. He too sent me a letter and said we should get together for a beer some time. We haven't got around to doing that but it was a nice thought.

The old house in Kiandra was getting a bit beyond me so I moved down to Talbingo. Of course, the old Talbingo Pub and the shady reaches along the Tumut River were now going underwater as Blowering Dam and then Jounama Pondage were completed. So it was the town built by the Snowy that I moved to. Just a couple of years later, the scheme was completed, with Tumut 3, the last of the Tumut power stations, now standing big and bold just up the river from town, beneath the huge wall of Talbingo Dam. The earthworks and cuttings that went into building that dam were massive. The Snowy really did move mountains. But beyond all the new scars, big old Talbingo Mountain stood out and gave me succour, reminding me that the peaks and the bush were still there despite all the change and the loss.

I didn't leave the Snowy just because of my advancing years. It must seem inconsistent of me to have talked about my awakening to the bush and to the spiritual beliefs that I've described, then to have continued working in jobs like the Snowy, which so changed the mountains. Well, I guess it was. I was always aware of that and that's why I've mentioned my uneasiness at times, like I was a bit of a hypocrite, always trying to convince myself that the mountains would still be just as grand at the end. But my experience in life is that few of us ever live up to our ideals completely, though that hardly excuses us. Towards the end of those Snowy years, I thought more than once about the strange sound that I'd heard that day outside the store and whether it was some kind of sign from the wilds. Well, if it was, it didn't recur on the Snowy – you know, as if it might have been a warning to stop what I was doing. But maybe I didn't need it because I ended up making my own decision to finish anyway. The growing sense of not being true to myself was as painful as the physical pain of labouring.

Jack Bridle had spent most of his life around the Tumut River and when I moved to Talbingo, we became firm friends. He'd been born at Adaminaby just before the Great War, so he was a bit of a spring chicken compared to me. Jack would tell me what the Tumut River was like before the dams were built. The swift rapids, the quiet reaches, the willow-fringed holes and the platypus and the kingfishers and the like. I'd talk to him about old Kiandra and the times I'd had in the mountains. Although Jack was a bit younger than me, in a sense we were both old men living in the past and struggling to cope with the present.

Jack was a keen fisherman, so he and I did a few trout fishing trips along the reshaped river. Despite the Snowy's changes, and the Tumut River that now was either flooded into lakes by the dams or a raging torrent where it still ran when they let water out for irrigation downstream, we could still find a few surviving nice spots. We had our favourite spinners and usually caught a few nice pan-sized browns or rainbows. On one occasion, we had to cross a bull paddock to get to the river. Jack knew the owner, so there wasn't a problem with access.

That is, except for the bull. As we slinked across the paddock hoping Mr Hereford wouldn't notice us, of course he did. He started to step slowly toward us, then increased speed to a trot, then went into full bellowing gallop. Here we were, two men – one in his sixties and the other in his eighties – trying to outrun a bull! I limped to the fence above the riverbank but got my rod tangled in the wires. Jack's behind me saying, 'Quick, Les, quick!' I just got the rod untangled, got myself through the fence, and then Jack got through, when the bull screeched to a halt at the fence with froth streaming from his mouth and nostrils. It was a close-run thing, that's for sure! But we did get a nice pair of trout at that spot. It was a good tale to share over a beer afterwards. Jack was a great storyteller as well as a bush poet, so an experience like that was fodder for his creativity.

The other thing we shared was a passion for the harmonica. Jack had played for years and I could keep up with him on most tunes. We started playing at the country club when they had dances on Saturday nights and it brought back memories of those south coast nights with Bruce and the band all those years ago. When Slim Dusty toured the mountains in the early 1970s, we were put on the bill with him at the club. Slim had been doing his annual round-Australia tour for a few years now and everyone in Talbingo was excited by Slim's decision to include the little place in his musical meander that year. For me, it was certainly an honour to be on the same stage as Slim, but one which saw me practising noon and night for a fortnight before. Luckily, with Jack's experience, he helped the two of us have a wonderful night, playing with the king of Australian country music. Slim was a nice fella. His wife Joy was a very good singer-songwriter in her own right and she treated us most warmly.

One day, I heard a vehicle pull up outside my little cottage. I wasn't expecting anyone, so I was a little surprised to see it was Jack. Not that I minded or anything; he was always welcome.

Jack came to the door with a troubled look on his face and said, 'Have you heard the park people are pulling Kiandra down?'

I said, 'What?'

Jack didn't have any more details, so said how about we drive up there. So I grabbed my hat and my stick, got into Jack's Holden and we headed up the highway, for such was the old road now. As we crested Gooandra Hill, we got our first glimpse toward distant Kiandra. I was horrified to see wisps of smoke rising from the town.

After about ten minutes, we arrived. The church was just a pile of fallen boards and iron. The old post office that the Paterick family had run for years was no more. Several other buildings were just piles of rubble. Around us, workmen levered with crowbars and hammers, every so often a wall would fall, and there was the clatter of debris being thrown into trucks for removal.

I spied a ranger in uniform and introduced myself. 'What the heck are you doing?' I said.

The ranger was an American named Russell. 'Well, Les, the old town is pretty much a ruin. Most of the really historic parts have long gone. There are other old gold towns in the state and it's been decided to let this one go. But we are keeping a few buildings.'

I replied, 'This is still a town. I was born here. Other people were born here, and died here. Whole families lived here. This was home for many people that I've known most of my life. Why is Kiandra less important than those other gold towns? Where else did miners put up with snow like they did here for years and years?'

'Well, we're just doing our job,', said Russell.

I was about to say something more when another ranger walked up to us.

He interjected, 'The place is a bit of an eyesore. It'll only be vandalised.'

With that, I poked him in the chest with my walking stick. 'You are the vandals,' I exclaimed.

He took a step back, a bit worried about what I might do next.

Jack placed a hand on my arm and gave me a wink, as if to say, 'Easy, Les.'

I looked up to Poverty Hill, where a column of smoke indicated all too clearly what had happened to our old home. Jack and I walked a little way further along the main street. Dad's old store was just a pile of chimney bricks – everything else was either gone or burnt. A few buildings were being retained: Jim and Fanny Pattinson's house up Pollocks Gully, the Wolgal Lodge, Harvey's hotel, which was now closed but used by snow-clearing teams in winter, and a little cottage owned by Bill Matthews. But it wasn't much. The smoke from the fires rose straight up into the air. It was one of Kiandra's very rare windless days.

I've rarely cried in my life. But that day, tears came very close to the surface. Distressed and disheartened, Jack and I got back into the car and drove home to Talbingo. Neither of us spoke the whole way.

Letters to the park superintendent, and to the local member, achieved little. Kiandra, or the Kiandra that I had known, was pretty well gone. I had come to see the park (it was called a national park by now) as a good progression in the mountains. We had to keep the mountains and all the things that lived there, and I knew that the park staff were very dedicated. But the destruction of Kiandra as part of the park's overall plan was just something I couldn't understand. What about history, wasn't that part of the mountains too? Didn't Kiandra deserve a place in the new scheme of things? It was one of the most disappointing events I ever experienced. I don't think I will ever understand quite why the Kiandra people's story was eradicated from the landscape in that way. Ranger Russell said that day that they would put up a sign telling tourists that Kiandra had been there, and that it was once a goldfield. He was taking away the town, and replacing it with a town sign. The irony of that was as bitter as the ash in the air.

43

I stayed on in Talbingo for a few years but my health started to deteriorate. The shock of that day at Kiandra took its toll on me. My right leg played up more and more, and the old ticker gave a flutter now and again, which left me a bit weak. So I moved down here to Tumut. Like Dad and Mum, it looks like I too am going to see my last years in this town. Things could be worse, could be a lot worse. It's a friendly place, and the hills and the river flats are a pleasant backdrop to the town. The river rushes along full of Snowy water for the irrigators out west.

We call this place a nursing home but it's really just a few rooms at the back of the hospital. There's a handful of us elderly folk here, apart from me. There's George, Muriel, Eileen and Noeleen (we call those two the Een Sisters), plus Cecil, who moved in here just the other day. They're all from around the district. We play a few hands of cards, talk about old times, and if the others dig me in the ribs often enough, then I'll play a tune for them on the old mouth organ. Jack visits every fortnight or so and plays a tune with me. The others call us the Harmonica Brothers.

I'm the last of the Leongs now. Belle passed away a year ago. She was a good sister to me and a good mother to her kids. They've all got good jobs and their own children have pretty well grown up now. Belle's husband Terry misses her terribly, judging from his letters, which I receive a few times a year. He and Belle were a good partnership and they obviously loved each other deeply.

Pete, sadly, had to move out of Belle and Terry's place some years back as he was getting just too much to handle. Belle found a place for him in a church-run home for mentally disabled people and Pete saw out his last years there. He died in his sleep two summers back last February 1st.

I had little contact with Mary over in New Zealand, but we did exchange the odd letter. Her husband Hilton died young and never did find the nugget that he dug for over so many years. Mary had better luck and won a small lottery prize, which helped her at last get her own home, as she and her hubby had always rented. She moved to the South Island, somewhere around Timaru, and lived there until last winter, when I was notified by the police that she had died of pneumonia. From the letters, I'd say she had a happy life. Never had any kids, but she and Hilton had a few adventures along the way. She never remarried, so I guess that indicates Hilton still lived on in her memory and she didn't want another man in her heart.

Jim, as I've said, turned into an unfortunate sort of bloke up in the north. He got on the grog and was repeatedly in trouble with the law. Finally he was shot by police in some sort of altercation outside a Darwin store. Apparently, Jim was arguing with the store owner about the price of a croc skin that Jim was trying to sell. A sad end for a good boy from Kiandra.

Much of the time I spend thinking about the years and how they have passed so quickly. You think life is stretching out in front of you, then all of a sudden it all seems behind you and you're looking back, wondering where the time has gone. But I'm thankful for the life that I've had. It has been a very good life, and I treasure all the things I've experienced and all the things I've learnt, both the good and the bad. I have lived and worked in a beaut part of Australia, a place that is still wonderful, despite all the changes. I still worry a bit about how I've been a part of those changes, but we have to earn a livelihood and I've tried to do that with respect for what was around me.

I will die knowing that nature, the mountains and the wild are very fine things, and hoping that as this nation and its people continue on their way they will find a way to live in harmony with those things. The land is powerful, and for those of us who feel it, whether blackfellow or whitefellow, or both like me, a life lived close to it offers many rewards. I can't explain all the things I've experienced, like some of the stranger things I've described to you. But perhaps it's good that it should be that way. Perhaps it's good that we don't know everything, and that a little bit of mystery should remain in everyone's life.

Jack will be here soon and I'm looking forward to the little drive that we'll do together. Probably we'll follow the route we usually do, up to Blowering Dam. From the dam wall, I'll be able to look way to the south, way up into the Tumut River valley, way up towards the mountains, and towards old Kiandra. I won't see the old place again, but it will be good to revisit it in memory. Yes, I'm looking forward to that little drive with Jack.

Author's note

Les Leong is a fictional character and his life is a fictional one. Having said that, there are some real people in this book and some real events. But the work is a novel, not a history. My work as an historian has assisted me to write the book and to create Les and his life. Other writers, historians, poets and interviewers whose work has been of assistance include Francis Harvey, Klaus Hueneke, Barry McGowan, D.G. Moye and Jane Ulman. Dean Freeman offered helpful advice. The art of Kim Young, Edgar A. Holloway and some unnamed artists inspired some of the chapter drawings (which, as you've no doubt guessed by now, were done by the same person who created Les). Various photographs by me and others helped inform several of the drawings too.

Some of the more graphic stories, though appearing like completely imagined ones, are in fact based on actual events. Vince Gollings having his head burnt off in his hut is based on the fate of Kiandra and Four Mile miner Bill Glennie; the story of 'John B' and the calf is based on court records from another NSW goldfield of the same period. Elements of the Smithers family saga are based on real events in the mountains. Several of the stories in the Kellys Plain section of the novel are based on actual events, some with real names, others with imagined ones. Wherever real names are used in this book, they are done so with respect for those people, one or two of whom I knew.

Author Elyne Mitchell and parliamentarian husband Tom drove by Jeep across the mountains in 1948. Les's 'yowie experience' is inspired by the Webb brothers' report in the *Queanbeyan Observer* of 7 August 1903.

Regarding frontier conflict, this region is often written of as having been 'quiet', or at least lacking in the killing of Indigenous people during initial white settlement. However, given that there was spearing of cattle, that the Franklins were originally forced out of the Brindabella valley by Aborigines, that Henry Hall shot and wounded Ngambri warrior Onyong for cattle spearing, that when Onyong died of unrelated causes his grave near Tharwa was desecrated by another white settler, and given that massacres occurred to neighbouring nations like the Wiradjuri, the 'quiet' tag is perhaps naïve. To suggest in a work of fiction that unrecorded killings occurred is not unreasonable.

The Lake Wonga community is entirely fictional and should not be confused with any present-day Indigenous communities on the NSW south coast.

Sadly yes, the NSW National Parks and Wildlife Service demolished most of historic Kiandra in the early 1970s. William Dobell and Mick Jagger did stay at Palfrey's hotel.

www.ingramcontent.com/pod-product-compliance
Lightning Source LLC
Chambersburg PA
CBHW071525100726
47908CB00004B/1296